THE
LAST
DARK
PLACE

THE
LAST
DARK
PLACE

AN ABE LIEBERMAN MYSTERY

STUART M.
KAMINSKY

 A TOM DOHERTY ASSOCIATES BOOK
NEW YORK

THE LAST DARK PLACE

This book is printed on acid-free paper.

A Forge Book
Published by Tom Doherty Associates, LLC
175 Fifth Avenue
New York, NY 10010

www.tor.com

Forge® is a registered trademark of Tom Doherty Associates, LLC.

Library of Congress Cataloging-in-Publication Data

Kaminsky, Stuart M.
    The last dark place : an Abe Lieberman mystery / Stuart M. Kaminsky.—1st ed.
        p. cm.
    "A Tom Doherty Associates book."
    ISBN 0-765-30463-5 (acid-free paper)
    EAN 978-0765-30463-6
    1. Lieberman, Abe (Fictitious character)—Fiction. 2. Police—Illinois—
Chicago—Fiction. 3. Prisoners—Crimes against—Fiction. 4. Chicago (Ill.)—
Fiction. 5. Extradition—Fiction. 6. Jewish men—Fiction. 7. Arizona—Fiction.
I. Title.

PS3561.A43L48 2004
813'.54—dc22

                                                                            2004047198

First Edition: December 2004

Printed in the United States of America

0   9   8   7   6   5   4   3   2   1

FOR PAUL BERGIN
FOR HIS LOVE AND KNOWLEDGE
OF THE MYSTERY
AND FOR HIS FRIENDSHIP

With a long leap from high above and dead drop of
weight I bring foot's force crashing down to cut the
legs from under the runner, and spill him to ruin.

—Aeschylus, *The Eumenides*

THE
LAST
DARK
PLACE

July 16, 1969

The little old man was nodding his head and mumbling to himself as he walked down the gray corridor of the synagogue. It was not an unusual sight, but this particular old man was unfamiliar to Morrie Greenblatt, who approached him.

Morrie towered over the old man, who wore a black yarmulke atop his freckled, nearly bald head and a white-fringed *tallis* over his shoulders. Under his arm the old man was carrying a black prayer book.

From the main sanctuary, the sound of voices, a man and a woman, went back and forth nervously.

"Excuse me," said Morrie.

The old man stopped and looked up at the tall slope-shouldered man who had stopped him.

"We need you," Morrie said, glancing at his watch.

"Me?" asked the old man in a voice that sounded raspy from too many hours of prayer.

"We need one more for the morning minyan," Morrie said. "A tenth man."

"But I . . . ," the old man began, looking toward the main sanctuary.

"It won't take long. I promise. Prayers and then if you have time we have bagels and coffee. We need you. Sid Applebaum was supposed to be here but he has a stomach something and with the rain . . ."

"You need me?" the old man said.

"Yes."

The old man shrugged and said, "Then I'll come."

Ten Jewish men who had been bar mitzvahed at the age of thirteen were required to meet the minimum number set forth in the Holy Bible for morning prayers. Morrie, who owned a bath and tile store on Lawrence Avenue, was the congregation's unofficial *gabai*, the one who saw to it that things got done.

No one, not even Morrie, was sure whether Morrie had volunteered for this job or it had simply evolved. Morrie, now almost fifty, accepted the responsibility, the principal task of which was to see to it that there was a minyan for each morning's prayers.

The regulars, if they were healthy, were no problem. He could always count on Rabbi Wass and his son, Cal Schwartz, Marvin Stein, Hyman Lieberman, Joshua Korn-pelt, Sid Applebaum, and himself. He would check the night before with phone calls and if it looked as if they would be short, Morrie would ask Marv Stein to bring his brother or Hy Lieberman to bring his sons. Some days they had as many as sixteen or more. Some days they had walk-ins who were from out of town or regular congregation members there to observe *yahrzeit*, the anniversary of a loved one's death.

When he had counted this morning, Morrie had been sweating. Both of Lieberman's sons had come, looking none-too-happy to be there. Maish Lieberman explained that their father Hyman wasn't feeling well. Maish was thirty-six and by this time in the early morning was usually at the T&L, the new deli he had opened with a loan from his father and Sid Applebaum. Abe, at thirty, was the puzzle of the lot. Short and lean like his father with the same dark curly hair, Abe was a policeman who came to services only when his father pressured him into doing so. Only last week Abe had been promoted to detective and an unimposing detective he was, a shrimp beanstalk with a sad face too old for his years. A few minutes ago, Maish, his yarmulke perched precariously atop his head, had nodded and talked about the price of eggs and the courage of astronauts. Abe in a sport jacket and tie looking like a shoe salesman had politely asked Morrie, "You want me to call Alex?"

"I'll find someone," Morrie had answered. It was a matter of pride, but time was against him.

"Alex can be here in ten minutes," said Abe.

"I'll find," Morrie had repeated.

"Morrie, this is my third day on the job. I've got to be downtown in an hour and a half."

"You'll be there," Morrie assured him. "The bad guys'll wait."

"Bad guys don't wait," Abe said. "Let me call Alex."

"I'll find," Morrie repeated. "With God's help, I'll find."

Abe Lieberman had shrugged and moved over to talk to Rabbi Wass's son, who at the age of thirteen was almost as tall as the policeman. The boy wore thin glasses that kept creeping down his nose. A sudden jab and they were back up again ready to start slipping.

Now, less than five minutes after he had left, Morrie

entered the small chapel across from the central sanctuary and announced,

"We have a minyan."

As Morrie ushered his treasured old man in, Marv Stein let out a loud sigh of relief. Marv was reliable, but he was also retired and Marv had a tee-off time in a little over an hour. God willing the rain would stop. "This is Mr. . . . ," Morrie began.

"Green," the old man said, taking Marvin's outstretched hand.

"Nice to meet you, Green," Marv said, and then added, "Let's get started."

The rabbi moved to the front of the small room, lectern before him, son at his side. The eight men and the rabbi's son sat in the chairs facing Rabbi Wass, a somber man with well-trimmed white hair, clean-shaven. To Abe, Wass looked like Lee J. Cobb with a stomachache.

Morrie smiled in relief, ready to lose himself in the comfort of daily prayer, looking forward to a poppy seed bagel with cream cheese and arguing with Josh Kornpelt on some point about the U.S. role in Vietnam and God's role in JFK's murder or why none of the astronauts were Jewish. They would move on to the Cubs' hope for a pennant next.

Green, the old man from the corridor, stood next to Morrie, who smiled at him. The Lieberman boys stood on the other side of the old man. Green gave a tentative smile back and the services began.

They didn't last long. Maybe five minutes. Maybe ten.

They were stopped by a loud, high-pitched raspy voice behind them. Not a shout but a high-pitched insistent demand.

"Hold it," the man said.

Rabbi Wass stopped and looked up through the narrow aisle that separated the cluster of ten men.

All heads turned to the man who had entered. They saw a tall young man in dark pants and a black T-shirt. He was about twenty with long uncombed dark hair and bad teeth. He was carrying a gun.

He didn't look like an Arab. Morrie concluded that he was a drugged-out wanderer who was there to rob them. Just so he wasn't an Arab terrorist.

"We are at prayer," said Rabbi Wass guiding his son, who had run to his side, behind him.

"You think I'm fucking blind," said the man, pointing his gun at the rabbi. "I can see what you're doing. I know where I'm at. I didn't think I was at the damned Dominick's supermarket or some shit."

The gunman shook his head and looked around at the men who had turned to face him. There was no doubt that the intruder was drunk, on drugs, or insane, possibly all three.

"You can have our money," Rabbi Wass said calmly.

"I know I can have your money," the tall man said, closing the door behind him. "I can have your money, your shirts, your shoes. I can have your goddamn lives."

He looked into each face before him growing more agitated.

"I don't want your goddamn money," he said willing himself, without success, to be calm. "Maybe I just want to come in here and let you know Jesus is coming and your asses are not getting into heaven. Don't matter how much you pray. You're going to hell."

"We shall take your opinion for what it is," said the rabbi, who had now completely shielded his son with his body.

"You're boning me," said the man with the gun.

"Boning you?" asked the rabbi.

"Making fun of me."

"I'm not in a position to make fun of you," said the rabbi.

"You're goddamn straight not in a position," the man said. "You are not in a position. Which one of you is Lee-burr-man?"

"Why?" asked the rabbi.

"I don't have to tell you why," the man said, stepping down the aisle. "I've got the gun. Just which one of you is Lieberman?"

"What do you want with Mr. Lieberman?" asked the rabbi.

The man with the gun shook his head.

"What do I want with him? I want to blow his damn head off. That's what I want with him. Now let's get it down and done and I'll get out of here."

"Why?" asked Rabbi Wass.

Someone was praying softly. Cal Schwartz. Cal was over eighty. His eyes were closed and he was gently swaying.

"What's he saying?" the gunman demanded.

"It's Hebrew," said Morrie. "He is saying that God is Almighty. That there is but one God and that His will *will* be done."

"Jesus, you people," said the gunman. "Lieberman, which one are you?"

"Why do you want to kill Mr. Lieberman?" asked Rabbi Wass again.

"Okay," said the man. "I got out of prison last week. I went home. I found out my little brother was dead. Over a year dead. A cop named Lieberman had shot him when Lance was just minding his own business. They kept it from me, told me Lance was away or some shit. Then I find out. I ask my mom where's Lance and she says, 'Connie, he was killed by some Jew in a uniform, killed for doing nothing, for being in the wrong place minding his own business.'"

"What makes you think Lieberman is here?" asked the rabbi.

"Because I'm no fucking dummy," said the man, tapping the barrel of his gun against the side of his head. "He's right in the phone book. I went to his apartment, brushed my hair back, smiled, and said to the woman who opened the door that I was an old friend of Lieberman. Little girl was standing next to her. The woman told me Lieberman was here. Short walk. Big gun."

"I'm Lieberman," Abe said.

"I'm Lieberman," Maish said.

And, not to be outdone and having seen *Spartacus* twice, Morrie said, "I'm Lieberman."

Then, one by one, each of them, even Mr. Green, who had been brought in as a stray from the hall, identified himself as Lieberman. The only ones who didn't were the rabbi and his son.

"All right then," the man with the gun said, "I can shoot all of you."

"You ever shoot anyone, Connie?" asked Abe.

The man looked at him, cocked his head to one side, and leveled the gun toward the thin young man who had asked the question.

"If there's got to be a first time," the man said, "it should be for good reason. I've got good reason."

"To kill eight, ten people?" asked Maish.

"If need be," said the gunman. "If need be."

"And if we rush you?" asked Kornpelt. "We get you. You shoot one, maybe two of us and you probably don't get Lieberman. You get the electric chair or life in jail is what you'll get."

"You're Lieberman," the gunman said to Joshua Kornpelt.

"I already told you I was," said Joshua.

The gunman was looking decidedly nervous now, his fingers clasping and unclasping the weapon in his head.

"I'll start with you," he said to Maish. "I shoot you. Odds are I've got the right guy. If not, Lieberman can let me know now who he is. How about them apples, Lieberman? I'm going to shoot big mouth now unless you step up like a man."

Maish tried to move past his brother to the gunman. Abe barred his way with his hand and stepped past Mr. Green and Morrie into the narrow aisle between the chairs.

"If you shoot any one of us," Abe said, "we'll all tell you that you shot Abe Lieberman. And we may be telling you the truth. Odds are eight to one you're wrong. Or maybe you're right. You kill another one of us and you still won't know. You said we're all going to hell. What about you? You kill innocent people and Jesus'll take you to heaven on a big white bird?"

"I'll repent," the gunman said.

"You'll be lying," said Lieberman. "You think Jesus won't know you're lying?"

"Shut up," shouted the gunman, pushing the gun inches from Abe's nose. "I'm starting with you. Right now."

"I'm Lieberman," Abe said.

"You're a smart-ass Jew, probably a lawyer."

"I'm Lieberman," Abe repeated.

"You armed?" the man answered.

"We don't wear guns in the synagogue," said the rabbi.

"You have a last name, Connie?" asked Lieberman. "If you're going to shoot me, I think I've got the right to know your name."

"You have the right? And what right did Lance have? Lance Gower. Remember him? You're Lieberman? Prove it."

The solution to this confused man's problem was evident

to Morrie. Just tell everyone to pull out his wallet and show his driver's license. But Connie the gunman, Connie the intruder was clearly not operating within the realm of reason.

The gun was now aimed at Lieberman's right eye. Lieberman blinked wearily.

"Your brother Lance had just beaten a pharmacist nearly to death. Your brother Lance had a Kmart bagful of money and drugs in one hand and a gun bigger than yours in the other. The pharmacist hit the alarm before he passed out. My partner and I got there as your brother was coming out of the store. He shot at us. We shot back."

"Bullshit and a half," the gunman sputtered, his face turning crimson. "Bullshit and a half. Lance was a good kid."

"The pharmacist nearly died. He still can't talk so you can understand him," said Lieberman.

"I will have my revenge. A life for a life."

"I prefer 'Live and let live,'" said Lieberman. "Or 'Vengeance is mine saith the Lord.'"

"I know the Good Book from cover to cover and back again," the gunman said. "I had seven years behind the walls. I read it. Now I've made a promise to myself, to Jesus, to my dead brother. I made a vow. Moses said, 'If a man vow a vow unto the Lord, or swear an oath to bind his soul with a bond, he shall not break his word, he shall do all that proceedeth out of his mouth.'"

The gunman looked around the men proudly. He could outdo these Jews with his eyes closed, outdo them with their own Bible.

"I took an oath," he said. "And I mean to keep it."

"'But if any man hate his neighbor, and lie in wait for him and rise up against him, and smite him mortally that he die, and fleeth into one of these cities," said Rabbi Wass. "Then the elders of his city shall send and fetch him thence, and deliver him into the hand of the avenger of blood, that he may die.'"

"Amen," said Morrie.

"Connie, let's go outside," Lieberman said to the gunman.

"Here suits me just fine," the man said. "I'm going to blow your head off right here. Mess up your walls and all of your memories the way I'm messed up about Lance."

Lieberman was in the aisle facing the man. Something touched Lieberman's back. He reached back slowly, keeping his sad eyes on those of the man with the gun whose bad breath wasn't overridden by the smell of alcohol.

"Mortal sin going down here," said Lieberman, taking from Maish's hand whatever it was he had poked Lieberman with.

"Maybe. Maybe not. That's the future," the man spat. "This is now. I'll be here tomorrow. You won't. I saw on the TV we're putting a man on the moon in a couple of days. Going to be right there live on television. Let me ask you. Are they sending NB-fucking-C TV up there to the moon? What the hell will you care? You'll be dead like my brother."

"One of the other astronauts, Collins, Murphy, something," said Morrie. "He'll have a camera."

The gunman's face was inches from Abe's now. He whispered, "Won't that be something to miss?"

The gunman saw a movement over Lieberman's shoulder. He stepped to the side just in time to see the rabbi's son duck through a door behind his father and slam it shut.

"Shit. Shit," said the gunman, shaking his head. "Now I gotta hurry. I didn't want to hurry. I wanted to stretch this, make you sweat, beg."

"We don't beg," said Maish.

"Give me the gun, Connie," said Abe wearily. "We've got a service to finish. We all have to get to work or to our families."

The gunman stepped back, shaking his head and smiling. Then he started to laugh.

"You got balls for a Jew. I give you that. But you'll be making 'em laugh in hell in a minute."

Lieberman pulled his hand from behind his back holding the gun that Maish had pressed into it. The gun was small. Abe hoped it was loaded.

"Give me the gun," Abe repeated.

The gunman's mouth dropped open. He looked from the gun to the sad face of the thin policeman.

"Like hell," he said leveling his own weapon at Abe Lieberman. "Looks like we're in for stormy weather."

"I'm not waiting for it," said Lieberman. "Give me the gun."

"Can you beat that?" Connie the gunman asked, looking around at the frightened faces of the men about him. "Can you beat that? Hell, I might as well shoot. Maybe we'll both die. No way I'm going back inside the walls, back inside and no evening-up for my brother."

"Suit yourself," said Abe, unsure of the weapon in his hand, concerned that a wild bullet might kill someone else in the small sanctuary.

"A suggestion," said Rabbi Wass, behind Abe.

"It better be a goddamn good one," said the gunman, looking into Lieberman's eyes. "We got ourselves one hell of a situation here and running out of time."

"You put down your gun," Rabbi Wass said. "And Detective Lieberman lets you walk out. We all pretend you were never here. We thank God for having saved us and we pray to him to have mercy on you."

"And he'll have mercy on me, your God?"

Rabbi Wass shrugged.

"Our God will do whatever he wants to do. We ask. He does what he wants to do."

"Very damn reassuring," the gunman said. "Makes me feel all safe and comfortable. The hell with it."

He raised his weapon at Abe, who did the same to him.

"Let's get it on," the gunman said.

"You're *shickered*," said Marv. "Drunk."

"If I wasn't, I couldn't be doing this," the man shouted.

"I'm going to shoot you in the eye," said Lieberman. "The right eye. That should be very painful, but it should work. You're shaking. You can't shoot straight and I'd say you haven't spent any time on the range. I've got a good chance of living and you've got a sure chance of dying. Think about it."

The gun wavered in the man's hand. He chewed on his lower lip and considered his fate.

"Hell," he said with a sigh. "I can't see Lance coming in here and doing this for me. He was always a selfish little prick, but don't tell my mom I said it."

He backed toward the door.

"Stop," said Lieberman. "Drop the gun."

The man turned his weapon quickly away from Abe, aiming it at Rabbi Wass.

"I'm going," he said. "Or I'm going to kill a priest."

"I'm a rabbi," said Rabbi Wass. "We haven't had priests for almost two thousand years."

Odds were, Lieberman calculated, that at this distance and shaking drunk the man with the gun might not hit Rabbi Wass. But then again, he might.

Abe watched as the man stepped back to the door through which he had come, fumbled at the handle and opened it.

"Forget I was here," he said. "I'll find a better time." He

was looking at Abe now. "I'll come back sober. I'll come to your apartment. Your wife's got a baby growing in her. I'll come and pay your family a visit. Think about that. Lance wasn't much but he was my brother and I got to live with myself."

"Who says?" said Morrie.

The man with the gun went through the door and slammed it behind him.

Abe ran to the door hearing the voices behind him, hearing his brother shout, "Abe, wait."

Abe didn't wait. He went through the door. The gunman was running awkwardly down the synagogue's hallway toward the front door. Across the hall, the door to the main sanctuary was open. A group of men and women were talking in front of the small platform, the *bimah*, setting up flowers. One of the women turned and looked at Lieberman and the gun in his hand.

Abe, tallis flying like a cape, yarmulke held down by his free hand, charged after the fleeing man who was now out the door and into the morning. The man looked, ran to his left and momentarily out of sight. Abe followed into a light morning drizzle.

The man was running more slowly now, drunk, out of shape. He looked back at Abe, who leveled his weapon. There was no one on the street. People inside the houses adjoining the synagogue were just waking up. Abe was aware of a few cars moving down the street.

"Stop," Abe called, not exactly a shout, more like a resigned call.

The man stumbled forward, turned and fired a shot that went in the general direction of the dark clouds. Abe fired back. The bullet from the small gun hit the concrete sidewalk a few feet behind the now gasping man.

The man turned, breathing heavily, and lifted his gun. It was hard to read the look on his face, confusion, hate, maybe a little self-pity. Abe fired again and the man tripped backward and fell, his gun leaping from his hand and skittering down the sidewalk away from him.

Abe stepped forward and stood over the fallen man.

"My leg," he said. "Damn, I picked the wrong day to do this."

"Want your gun back?" Abe said evenly, aiming his weapon at the man's face.

"My gun? I want an ambulance, a doctor. You shot me in the goddamn leg. I'm bleeding to death."

"I'll give you your gun back and shoot you in the face if that will make you feel better," said Abe, hearing voices behind him coming out of the synagogue. "No more pain."

"A doctor," the man said.

Abe knelt next to the man and said, "I'm not a religious man, but that" — glancing back at the synagogue — "is where my father and brother pray, where my friends and their families feel safe. You made it dirty. You went to where I live and you came here and threatened my wife and daughter. I take umbrage at that. Can you blame me?"

The man looking up at him shook his head "no."

Footsteps were moving quickly toward the detective and the gunman now.

"I'm calling an ambulance and I'm having you booked and when you get out, don't come here or anywhere near my home, my family, or my brother's family. You understand? No questions. No discussions. I'll kill you."

The man nodded, looking over Lieberman's shoulder at the men hurrying toward them, *tallises* flying, a flock of Jewbirds swooping down on their prey.

"I understand," the man said, closing his eyes. "It hurts. It goddamn hurts."

"It's supposed to. It'll hurt for a few years," said Lieberman, standing. "Then it'll go away. One more thing, Connie. I didn't shoot your brother. I was there but another cop did it."

"Why didn't you just say that in there?" the man groaned.

"Would you have believed me?"

"No," said the man, gritting his teeth, blood streaming from his leg.

"You believe me now?"

"No, yes. I don't know. My leg."

"Abe," Maish called behind him. "Are you all right?"

"Fine," said Abe, moving to pick up the gunman's fallen weapon by the barrel. "Someone call an ambulance and the police."

"My son already called the police," said Rabbi Wass.

"I'll call an ambulance," said Morrie, scurrying back to the synagogue.

Abe looked at the men who had come to help him: Josh Kornpelt, Marv Stein, and behind them old Cal Schwartz and the tenth man Morrie had pulled from the corridor, Mr. Green. They were shuffling forward clutching their prayer books. Rabbi Wass moved to the fallen, moaning intruder.

"A gun in the synagogue?" Abe said to his brother reproachfully.

"When did I ever have a gun?" Maish said, pointing to himself, his droopy face looking hurt.

"It's mine," said Green.

"He handed it to me," said Maish. "I passed it to you."

Abe looked at the old man.

"You have a permit for this?"

"I was a cop," said Green. "Long time ago, but I was a cop. I got a permit."

Abe was about to ask another question when he saw a tall, thin woman in her late thirties come running out of the synagogue holding a black hat on her head with the palm of her hand. The woman was heading for the men and screaming, "Pop."

They all turned to watch her join them. Her hair was red, her eyes green and frightened. She looked at Abe who held two guns, at the fallen man, and at Mr. Green.

"I'm a police officer," Abe said.

"He is," said Rabbi Wass.

"Pop," the woman said to Green. "What's going on? What happened to you? You go to the bathroom and get lost and then I find you out on the street with guns."

"They needed me," said Green.

"For what?" she asked. "We're here for Dolly's son's confirmation."

"Bar mitzvah," said Marvin. "It's called a bar mitzvah."

"That's why we're here," she said, ignoring Marvin.

"I know," said Green. "But they needed me."

"For what?" the woman demanded.

"Prayers," Green said proudly. "They need ten men for prayers."

"They need ten Jews for prayers, Pop. Ten Jews. You're Catholic."

"They needed me."

"My father's name is Patrick Ryan Green," the woman said in exasperation to the men around her as the drizzle stopped. "He doesn't count."

"I think he does," said Maish.

"Let's get to Dolly's boy's confir—bar mitzvah," she said, taking her father's arm and leading him back toward the synagogue.

The man stopped abruptly and faced Abe.

"Is it always like this?" Patrick Green asked.

"Not always," said Abe.

"When are you doing it again?"

"Tomorrow," said Maish.

"Can I come back?" asked Green.

"Anyone's welcome," said Marvin.

"Amen," said Cal Schwartz.

"Pop," the woman said, rolling her eyes and leading her father away.

"I'll get the gun back to you," called Abe. "Thanks."

Green looked over his shoulder, smiled, and said, "I'll pick it up tomorrow."

Thirty-Three Years Later

Lieberman stood in the food court of the Yuma airport trying to decide if there was anything there he could eat that wouldn't be bad for him.

He was hungry.

His cholesterol was high. The burning of a future ulcer played his stomach lining like a mandolin. There was almost nothing he could safely eat.

He was hungry.

"Hungry?" he asked the men at his side.

The nearest one, Connie Gower, was taller than Lieberman, heavier, darker, and far more sullen. In thirty years, Gower had lost all his teeth, installed large white ones, cut his hair, and clicked off at least eight mob hits and who knows how many freelance killings. His hair was white, cut short and he always wore a solid turtleneck shirt under a sports jacket. It had become his trademark.

Lieberman had no trademark. He stood five-foot-seven, weighed 140 pounds, was white of hair, had the face of a sad beagle, and looked a decade older than his sixty years.

He reached up to touch his mustache and considered his dietary options. They were glum and he was handcuffed to Gower, which didn't make things better because Connie was definitely in need of a shower. With his right hand, Lieberman grasped a small carry-on, which contained two changes of everything, his toiletries, a paperback copy of *Theodore Rex*, and a locked metal box. He had put the cuff on Connie's right hand and his own left so Lieberman could reach under his jacket for his gun if Connie decided to do something stupid, which was not likely, but Connie was desperate and had a few hundred reasons for not wanting to go back to Chicago.

The primary reason wasn't even that there was a warrant for his arrest for murder. He could probably beat that. Connie had a short sheet. Besides the terrorizing of Abe's synagogue thirty years earlier, he had only one other conviction, for carrying a concealed weapon without a license. No, what concerned Connie was the people for whom he had committed the most recent murder and, if it came to it, his other past clients whom he might turn evidence on to cut a deal with the Cook County state attorney, which was why Lieberman's six-shot .357 Smith & Wesson revolver was tucked into the holster under his jacket. A week earlier he had passed the annual qualification with the weapon with twenty-eight of thirty shots "in the box" at five-, ten-, and thirty-feet ranges.

Lieberman had come to Yuma because Connie Gower had fled Chicago where he was wanted for murder. Lieberman had fed information on Gower into the LEADS, the national law enforcement computer network, and had sent information to the Federal Bureau of Investigation and the FBI Fugitive Task Force. Gower had been picked up in Yuma after a traffic accident and the Yuma police had identified him as a fugitive. Abe had obtained an Unlawful Flight to Avoid Prosecution warrant according to Detective Division Special Order 02–03 and filed it with LEADS.

The man on the other side of Connie was Yuma detective Martin Parsons, no more than thirty, lean, redheaded, neat-suited, and very serious. Parsons was accompanying them through security and onto the plane and no further.

Parsons was hungry but he was also anxious to get rid of this responsibility. Gower glanced around and said, "Let's just get on the fucking plane."

Lieberman held back a sigh. There would be nothing but pretzels or peanuts and coffee on the America West flight that would take almost six hours with a stop in Phoenix.

They didn't stop for food, but Lieberman did pause at a kiosk and pick up two Snickers bars. It would have to hold him. He had no intention of getting off the plane with his prisoner in Phoenix where they had a half-hour layover.

Lieberman's partner, Bill Hanrahan, would meet Lieberman and his prisoner when they got off the plane at O'Hare in Chicago. There was no place for Connie to run once they were on the plane and really no place to run before they got on unless he was going to drag Lieberman with him.

Now a man of Connie's size, who did not know the little Jewish cop, might consider his odds of simply ripping off the cop's arm, hitting the Yuma cop with it, and running. There were people in Chicago who wanted Connie dead and had a good track record of making people dead.

But Connie knew Lieberman not just from their encounter three decades earlier. Both men had reputations. Lieberman had earned his for being willing to do whatever was necessary to control a situation, even if that meant putting a large hole in a big man.

Lieberman had not shot as many people as Connie Gower. Current count was sixteen. He would have to have a good lawyer and a lot of luck to get a chance at seventeen. Connie had heard that Lieberman had shot five people, killing three of them.

That's what Connie was thinking in the food court in the Yuma airport at three in the afternoon, but Lieberman's mind had been on other things, namely, his hunger and how he and his wife Bess were going to come up with the ever-rising cost of his grandson Barry's coming bar mitzvah.

Connie would gladly have given the Chicago cop fifty thousand, cash, nothing traceable, just to turn the key on the cuff and look the other way. But Connie knew that wasn't going to happen.

The airport wasn't crowded. It hardly qualified as near empty. It had rained heavily, was still raining heavily. Flights had been canceled. Their flight to Chicago had been delayed. Lieberman was hungry. He wanted a kosher hot dog. He wasn't going to get one, not for a while. He considered pulling one of the Snickers bars out of his pocket and decided he would wait till they were safely seated on the plane.

There were wet spots on the floor. An old black man was mopping them. A man and woman in their fifties, the man with a belly, the woman without, were standing in front of the Burger King counter with two kids, both boys no more than ten and eleven, sulking behind them. One kid was poking the other in the chest with his finger and grinning. The poked kid was turning red. Of course, he was smaller. Lieberman wondered if the couple were the kids' parents or grandparents.

A few other people, two flight attendants, both lean

women in blue uniforms, hurried past talking. Both women were in their forties.

Lieberman followed the young cop through security after Parsons showed the uniformed security guard his identification. Security had been expecting the trio.

On the other side of the machine, through the arch, Lieberman opened his carry-on case under the eye of the heavyset black woman in a blue uniform who didn't even glance at the handcuffs or Connie. She stayed focused on Lieberman, who removed his weapon, placed it in the metal box, locked the box, put the box in the carry-on, tucked the key in his pocket, and zipped the carry-on. The woman nodded.

Lieberman, Parsons, and Connie moved on and a thin, white security checker said to the black woman, "That old guy's a cop?"

"Chicago," she said.

"They must be desperate in Chicago," he said with a shake of his head.

She smiled, looking at the three men about to turn the corner and head down the corridor toward their plane. The old cleaning man pushing his cart waved at the security man and the black woman, and moved around the gate. She waved at him and called, "How you doin', Billy?"

The old man nodded and waved back.

The two detectives and their prisoner were moving slowly. No hurry. There would have been time for a Whopper, a taco, a Big Mac, a chicken salad sandwich. Too late now. No crowds. It was Yuma, early morning. A pair of female flight attendants pulling carry-ons hurried past talking about having three hours in Chicago. A couple with two little kids, one an infant in her father's arms, the other a little girl no more than three or four with long curls and a pout, being pulled forward toward the gate by her mother, who wore a purple T-shirt with turquoise letters telling those who looked her way that she was *She Who Must Be Obeyed*.

A few people were seated by the gate watching the television monitor, which cooed Hawaiian-sounding music and showed a sandy beach. At the desk, the Yuma cop talked to the woman behind it, who nodded and moved to the door to the gangway.

Lieberman looked around under his droopy lids. He was unarmed but so was everyone else at the gate with the exception of Parsons.

Actually, that was wrong. One other person was armed. His name was Billy Johnstone. He was almost seventy. He was lean, black, and pushing a cleaning cart on which, under a towel, rested a gun. He stopped about a dozen feet from the three men, pulled a pair of glasses from the pocket of his gray uniform, perched them on his nose with shaking fingers, and reached under the towel.

Lieberman's eyes met those of Billy Johnstone. Recognition, not of the face of the man but of the face of a man who suddenly looked odd. No, it was more than "odd," it was frantic. Lieberman's hand started under the jacket for the weapon that wasn't there. Neither Parsons, the young cop, nor Connie Gower saw the old man with the gun. Lieberman shoved at Gower, knowing it was too late.

Billy Johnstone fired. Connie Gower jerked forward, pulling Lieberman with him. A second shot came and Connie went down. Lieberman tumbled forward and landed on his back.

Lieberman hit his head on the tile floor as a third and fourth shot were fired. When he looked up, the old man, no longer wearing glasses, was on his knees and Parsons was standing with his Ruger in two hands.

There was blood on the chest of the old man, who dropped the gun to the floor. Lieberman was aware of people screaming as the Yuma cop stepped forward and kicked the weapon, which had been dropped far beyond the reach or understanding of the old man, who slumped to his side, his eyes now searching out Lieberman.

The old man said something as Lieberman, on his knees, touched Connie's neck. Lieberman looked at the old man. Parsons was now standing over him.

"He dead?" asked Johnstone.

"He's dead," said the Yuma cop.

The old man smiled, closed his eyes, and rolled over on his back.

"He dead?" asked Lieberman, looking at the old man and searching his pockets for the key to the cuffs.

"No," said Parsons. "Not yet."

"Get an ambulance," Lieberman shouted at the woman behind the check-in desk. Her mouth was open and her face dead white.

And a hard drinking woman or a slow thinking man will
be the death of me yet.
   —"Hard Drinking Woman" by Lee Cole Carter

Wayne Czerbiak was sane. At least he was as sane as Monty
Giopolus who stood behind the second of three chairs at the
Clean Cut barbershop on Ridgeway in a small mall just off
Howard Street. Eight dollars for a haircut, three barbers, no
waiting. But sometimes there were only two barbers. Some-
times only one. Actually, there was usually only one, Monty.
It didn't matter. There was never much of a wait, if any, at
the Clean Cut.

  Wayne listened to Monty talk as Monty cut his hair.
Monty was a throwback. He had seen barbers in movies, old
movies where the barber just talks and talks. That was a
major reason Monty had become a barber. He liked to talk
about anything. Baseball, the market, the latest gossip about

drug abuse by some multimillion-dollar basketball player, Rhoda Brian's stomach stapling. You name it, Monty had an opinion or little-known information on the subject.

"Mayor's thinking of putting in a park right over there," Monty said, pointing through his shop window at an open space across the street. "It's too small. Kids should have room to move around. But you know what I say?"

He kept cutting but paused a beat so Wayne could respond by saying "What?"

Wayne said nothing, just sat and listened. Songs ran through his head, background music that fit the scene. For Wayne, the major factor in his becoming a sign painter was that his father had been a sign painter till arthritis crippled him and he turned over his brushes and paints to Wayne three years ago and died a year later. Wayne had a natural talent and it was easier to just paint signs than do what was necessary to become a doctor or something. The fact was that Wayne couldn't think fast on his feet. School had always been a puzzle he couldn't solve, a game whose rules he could never learn.

Besides, Wayne was proud of some of his work, the real challenges, like the sign he did a few months ago, black letters on yellow, Old English: PIECE OF CAKE, with a picture Wayne drew of a cake with white icing in a flowing, delicate pattern.

The cake was vanilla with cherries inside. You couldn't tell that by looking at the sign, but Wayne knew it. It was important to him to know things like that so he could make the cake look real. Without knowing what was inside, it was just a hollow shell.

Sometimes Wayne felt like a hollow shell. When that happened, he quickly filled the shell with food. He was thinking of a Big Mac while Monty kept talking.

"I say," said Monty, "that it's a payback to the alderman. Payback for things done, favors. You know what I mean?"

Wayne didn't answer. He was thinking of a Big Mac and how he was going to kill Lee Cole Carter.

Bringing Sean O'Neil to the T&L deli was probably a bad idea. They were sitting in the back booth, the third booth that was semi-reserved for the friends and family of Abe Lieberman's brother Maish, who owned and operated the T&L.

Bill Hanrahan was sitting in the booth, facing the door. He looked across the table at the detective who was shaking his head and looking at the lox, onion, and cream cheese omelet in front of him.

"What?" asked Hanrahan, a fork full of his own omelet almost to his mouth.

"I dunno," said O'Neil. "Jew food. I dunno. It doesn't go down right. Know what I mean? Something about it just doesn't go down right."

O'Neil was almost as big as Bill Hanrahan, who looked like the pro-football lineman he had almost been before the knee injury. O'Neil was about fifteen years younger than Bill, a few pounds lighter and a muscled weight lifter. Bill thought he could take the younger man on if it came to that. He didn't think O'Neil had the deep stomach. He could be wrong.

"No, what do you mean?" asked Hanrahan, chewing on a mouthful of omelet. "What doesn't go down right?"

People making their regular morning stop before heading for work filled the red leatherette swivel seats at the counter. At the eight-seat window table behind O'Neil, five old men were arguing loudly.

"Come on," said O'Neil, buttering his toasted bagel and nodding toward the loud old men. "Listen to them."

He turned his head to his right to indicate the group of old men. Hanrahan looked at the regular morning meeting of the *alter cockers*, all old Jews with the exception of Howie Chen, who was as old as most of them and spoke better Yiddish, the result of having owned a Chinese restaurant two blocks down on Devon for over forty years. Howie was a cousin of Hanrahan's wife Iris. Iris's father owned a Chinese restaurant on Sheridan Road. Hanrahan wondered what Sean O'Neil thought about the Chinese. Hanrahan's eyes met those of Morris Hurwitz, PhD, not the oldest, nor most outspoken or even the unofficial leader of the *alter cockers*, but definitely the smartest.

There was a fleeting contact of something like understanding between the Irish cop and the retired Jewish social worker. Herschel Rosen, the *cockers'* would-be comic, followed Hurwitz's eyes and said, "The Irish cop is here with reinforcements to protect him from the ancient mariners. When is Lieberman coming back?"

O'Neil made a face.

"Due back today," Hanrahan said above the low level of talk at the counter and the clatter of dishes as Maish waddled around, sad-dog faced, delivering plates of food.

Lieberman had introduced Bill to the T&L and the *alter cockers* four years ago. It had taken Hanrahan a few months to get used to the place, to the banter. The food he liked particularly, especially the herring in cream sauce.

"None too soon," said Red Bloomberg, who may have once been Irish-redheaded but was now bald. "How's your cousin, the mayor? He going to get my Justin that job in City Hall?"

Hanrahan was not the mayor's cousin, but the mayor was Irish.

"I'm working on it," Hanrahan said, reaching 1. coffee.

"Boy," said O'Neil. "Typical Jew crap, wanting special treatment. You related to Daley?"

"No," said Hanrahan after a sip of coffee. "And that old man knows it. It's a joke, a running joke. Friendly."

O'Neil, who had professed his dislike of the Jew food, was doing a good job at finishing his bagel and butter with a thin slice of Nova lox. He was almost through with his omelet.

"Funny," said O'Neil emotionlessly.

"Not the point," said Hanrahan. "He's making contact, showing everyone he knows a cop. It's not much but it makes him happy. The man's got colon cancer. It's slowly killing him."

"Tough," said O'Neil. "My dad died in Korea when a cook blew a hole in his back. Where was your Jew?"

Hanrahan put down his cup and felt his fists tightening. O'Neil was Irish. His face was pure beefy no-neck Irish, an Irish much like Hanrahan's father and, yes, Hanrahan himself.

"How about we talk about the case?" asked Hanrahan, unclenching his fists and finishing the last of his omelet.

Hanrahan's attention now turned to the bowl of herring in cream sauce he had been saving for last.

"You really going to eat that?" asked O'Neil.

"No, I'm just going to admire it," said Bill, plunging his fork into a large piece of herring.

O'Neil shook his head. A few weeks earlier he had been transferred to the Clark Street station from the Eighteenth, the East Chicago district a few blocks from Cabrini Green. When Lieberman went to pick up his prisoner in Yuma the day before, a bag lady had been killed in an alley on Sherwin.

Hanrahan had caught the case and Captain Kearney had assigned O'Neil to him till Lieberman returned.

Hanrahan would have preferred to take it as a 10–99 and work it alone, but Kearney had insisted on a two-officer unit, a 10–4.

Bill worked slowly on his herring.

"How about we get going?" said O'Neil. "I don't feel all that comfortable in here. You know what I'm saying? Like the Palestinians surrounded by them."

"Cut that shit," said Hanrahan.

"Shit?"

"About the Jews. Yesterday it was blacks and Hispanics."

"Niggers and spics," O'Neil corrected. "They didn't hear me."

"Not the point," said Hanrahan. "I heard you. I don't want to hear you again."

"About anything?"

"About racial crap. We sit right here and go over it. I finish what I'm eating. Then we go."

O'Neil shrugged. Maish brought them refills on the coffee. Maish, whose son had been murdered by a black Jamaican a few years earlier, held no anger against blacks or Jamaicans. Hanrahan knew that. Maish saved his rage and anger for God.

O'Neil sighed and pulled out his notebook.

"While you were thinking about being fucking politically correct," O'Neil said, looking at his notebook, "I talked to the uniform who found her. That's all right with you right? I mean you did tell me . . ."

"Fine," said Hanrahan, pouring cream into his coffee.

"And I went to see the body," O'Neil went on. "Talked to the ME. That all right with you, too?"

"When?"

"About four this morning. I hear you have a new wife. Didn't want to wake you before I had to. You know you could have been . . ."

"What did you find?" asked Hanrahan, certain now that he could not handle a full day with this son of a bitch, Irish or no Irish.

"You know that series of random beatings by a carful of teens?"

"The Twentieth, Foster District," said Hanrahan.

The beatings in the Ravenswood neighborhood where Bill lived were getting worse. There had been five of them. Witnesses had given some identification. No one had been killed. At least not before the bag lady.

But the bag lady had been killed in Bill's territory, the Twenty-fourth, the Rogers Park District.

"Wounds consistent with baseball bats like victims of the other beatings reported seeing," said O'Neil.

"No one saw this one," Hanrahan said. "How do you know it's the same . . ."

"Intuition," said O'Neil, biting his lower lip and winking. "Time of night matches. Wounds match. Nothing taken, at least nothing we know. Nothing taken in the other beatings either. Didn't look like she had anything worth taking, not even her life."

"The uniform who took the call with his partner opened a cup of hot, steamy, and delicious black coffee sold by a cross-eyed Indian with a cart who showed up to feed the crowd of gawkers. Very enterprising, those Indians."

Hanrahan stared at O'Neil, who smiled.

"Want to know what he said? The uniform?"

Hanrahan nodded.

"He thinks he may know who did it. Says he and his partner ran down a carful of kids a few nights ago. Ticketed the driver for running a red light. Kids were white. Anyway, my uniform, for whom I had bought coffee, does a search, checks the trunk. Want to know what he found?"

There were only two people left at the counter, but none of the *alter cockers* had left.

"Baseball uniforms and shoes in the trunk," said O'Neil.

"And bats," Bill guessed.

"Irish smarts," said O'Neil, tapping his own forehead.

"You got the driver's name?"

"And address." O'Neil pointed to his notebook.

Hanrahan's cell phone played the opening notes of "Danny Boy." He pulled it from his pocket and said, "Hanrahan."

"Father Murph, I've got a delay."

"What happened?"

"Gower's dead. Shot. Not by me. I'll fill in the holes later. I called Kearney. And Bess. It'll be another day."

"Keep in touch, Rabbi," said Hanrahan.

Lieberman clicked off. So did Hanrahan.

"Lieberman?" O'Neil asked.

Hanrahan answered, "Let's go."

They got up from the booth, paid the check, and heard Herschel Rosen call after them as they went through the door, "Go catch the bad guys, corned beef and cabbage. We'll hold down the fort."

"We'll man the barricades," said Hurwitz.

"Batten down the hatches," added Hy Glick.

Outside the sky was morning April-bright.

"The uniform who told you all this. He Irish?"

"Nope," said O'Neil. "A wop."

There was a soft blue-green fluorescent bulb over the head of the bed in the recovery room. The oscilloscope hummed and blipped quietly, creating green mountains and valleys on a black background.

Lieberman sat, cup of coffee in his hand, his eyes going from the thin black man in the bed to the screen.

The man in the bed had been shot in the chest. The wound, Lieberman has been told, was serious but probably not critical. The bullet, which broke a rib and grazed a kidney, has been removed and internal bleeding stopped.

His name was Billy Johnstone. He was almost seventy-one and, like Lieberman who was sixty-one, looked far older than his years. Johnstone's mouth was partly open, eyes closed, a tube through his left nostril. The hospital gown was open enough so Lieberman could see the chest of curly white hair slowly heaving in and out.

Lieberman drank some coffee. It wasn't bad. It wasn't good, but it was coffee. He wasn't supposed to drink caffeinated coffee. He didn't know if this coffee was decaffeinated. He didn't care. He sipped and remembered his Snickers bars. He put his cardboard cup on the nightstand, pulled a candy bar from his pocket, unwrapped one end and took a bite.

A uniformed Yuma police officer sat outside the closed door. Billy Johnstone wasn't going anywhere, not for a while, and then to jail to wait for the legal wrangling, a deal to be made, or prison time. This was Yuma's case, but Abe's prisoner had been killed and he needed to know why, not only to satisfy his own curiosity but also to put in his report, a report he definitely was not looking forward to writing.

Lieberman closed his eyes and heard a raspy thin voice say, "You got blood."

Lieberman looked at the man on the bed. His eyes were open but the lids were fluttering.

"Enough to keep me going," said Lieberman.

"No, I mean you got blood on your shirt there."

Johnstone tried to raise a bony arm to point at Lieberman's shirt.

"Sorry 'bout that," Johnstone said.

"It'll wash out."

"I know, but . . ."

"Want a Snickers bar?" asked Lieberman.

"Like 'em, but I don't think I'm supposed to eat anything," said Johnstone.

"You want to talk?" asked Lieberman.

"Not 'specially."

"Just a few questions."

The old man blinked his eyes and nodded, indicating a few questions would be about all he could handle.

"Why'd you shoot him?"

"He's dead? For sure?"

"He's dead."

The old man smiled and closed his eyes.

"Thought I'd be, too. That was the plan. He was a bad man, a killer, that right?"

"He was," said Lieberman. "That why you killed him?"

"Just felt like it."

"Just something to do on a rainy morning in Yuma," said Lieberman flatly. "Get a gun, sneak it into the airport, shoot a bad man."

"Something like that," Johnstone said.

"Someone paid you."

"Hmm. You a baseball person?"

"Yes," said Lieberman.

"Good. Two kinds of people. Baseball and not baseball. You know what I'm saying?"

"Yes."

"Back some forty-five years ago it looked like I might make it to the major leagues," Johnstone said. "You imagine that? Looking at me now, you imagine that?"

"Who'd you play for?"

"Kicked around some. Ended with a Red Sox Triple-A team. Thought I'd go up. Went down and out instead. My last season I drove in fifty-four runs and had a batting average of two-eighty right on the button, right on it. Got sent down. Just when things were lookin' right. Shot down. Sent down. Down and out."

"Why did you shoot the man in the airport?"

"You know I've got cancer of the liver and some other parts," Johnstone said.

"I'm sorry."

"Not half as much as I am," the old man said with a sigh.

"The question," said Lieberman.

"You got children?" He squinted at Lieberman and said, "Grandchildren?"

"A daughter. Two grandchildren."

"How old?"

"Twelve and nine. Boy's twelve. Girl's nine."

"I've got three. Grandchildren. Smart. College smart."

Lieberman was about to speak when Johnstone raised his right hand palm up for him to stop.

"Takes a lot of money to send kids to college," Johnstone said.

"A lot of money."

The man in the bed closed his eyes and was silent for about thirty seconds. Lieberman thought he was asleep, but with closed eyes Johnstone said quietly, "You see where I'm going with this?"

"I think so. Someone paid you a lot of money for you to kill Gower. You're going to give it to your grandchildren to go to college."

"A mind is a terrible thing to waste. Seen those ads?"

"I donate to the United Negro College Fund," Lieberman said. "Who paid you to shoot Gower?"

"So the man I shot was named Gower? First name or last?"

"Last."

"You had a photograph of Gower in your pocket."

"But not his name. Never knew his name till you just said it. You ever kill a man? I mean you being a cop?"

"A couple of times."

"Thought I'd feel bad," said Johnstone. "I do, but physical not mental. Ever been shot?"

"No. The person who hired you to kill Gower wasn't a good man," said Lieberman.

"Maybe so. Maybe no. But he was a man with money."

Johnstone leaned a little toward Lieberman and lowered his voice.

"Between you, me, and your Snickers bar, I already put the money where only my grandkids can get it. Add that to my insurance money and it's a nice amount. You can't take it from me."

The oscilloscope let out a series of blips. The green line was frantically drawing the dark landscape.

"I don't want to take your money. I want the name of the man who paid you."

"Can't do it," Johnstone said. "I think I better . . . there water in here?"

"I'll call the nurse. They told me not to give you water."

"But they didn't say anything about candy bars?"

"I'll call the nurse."

"No." He held up a thin arm, bone and veins showing. "No more talk now," Johnstone whispered and then he was definitely asleep.

Lieberman got up and moved toward the door. He would come back later.

"You understand?" Monty said.

Monty the barber looked like a twig, a bald twig with wide brown suspenders. Monty had blue eyes and peppermint breath. He popped Certs like Wayne's cousin Kenneth had popped uppers back in the eighties when they were kids.

"Yes," said Wayne looking at himself in the mirror, watching the hair fall in ringlets as Monty cut and talked, narrow knobby shoulders huddled holding today's suspenders.

The Clean Cut was old, ceiling a patterned plaster, floor white tile blocks with cracks that ran like meandering rivers, walls covered in paper with repeating pictures of ancient airplanes.

Monty was alone today. The other barber chairs sat empty and only Mr. Photopopolus, who lived in the Garden Gables Assisted Living Facility in a three-story off of Morse near the El, sat waiting. The bus had driven Mr. Photopopolus from the Garden Gables. It would be back for him in an hour. Mr. Photopopolus didn't care if it was five hours. He liked the smell of the barbershop. He liked fingering the curled edges of the magazines that flopped on the small table next to him. He liked listening to Monty and throwing in an observation when he could.

"So, it's a miracle," Monty said. "All this."

He paused to wave his comb and point it around the shop. Wayne could see him in the mirror.

"You gotta think about it, Wayne," he went on. "People were on the earth with nothing, nothing at all, no thing at all. Just people and the earth and the animals and whatever was growing. And they made from it houses and cars and computers and cake mixers."

"And streets and telephones and airplanes," said Mr. Photopopolus.

"I'm going to shoot someone today," said Wayne softly, looking at the elegant letters painted on the window more than forty years ago by his father saying this, indeed, was the Clean Cut barbershop.

"That a fact?" said Monty.

"Yes."

Monty had heard crazier things in his decades of scissors, razors, and combs. Wayne was harmless, a little off, but harmless. Customers babble. You listen, nod your head, let them tell you they were about to make millions or shoot the latest blond rock star.

"Something eating you?" Monty said.

"No, nothing special. It's just the day I'm going to shoot someone," said Wayne again, very softly, calmly, looking in the mirror to be sure Monty was cutting his hair just the way he liked it, not too short. Too short and his face looked like a balloon, like John Candy.

"You got to kill somebody, kill Dwight Spenser," said Mr. Photopopolus. "No loss there. You gotta kill somebody, kill Spenser, get it out of your system, rid the world of an anti-Greek. I thought a couple times about braining him with a bedpan."

"I don't know Spenser," said Wayne.

"Room next to mine," said Photopopolus. "Must be a hundred years old. God's keeping him alive to punish those around him who've screwed up their lives. I'm eighty-six. He'll outlive me. The bad die ancient. You know what I'm saying?"

"I know what you're saying," said Wayne. "But I've got to kill someone important."

"Like who?" asked Photopopolus.

"Lee Cole Carter," said Wayne.

"And that's who?" asked Photopopolus.

"Country singer," said Monty dreamily, still thinking about the miracle of the world, the wonders of a comb, the marvel of the scissors in his hand. "Mother and father live in one of the high-rises on Sheridan. Top floor I hear. Lee Cole Carter won the Grammy last year for singing something about dirty women."

"'Hard Drinking Woman,'" Wayne said. "Youngest country-and-western singer to win a Grammy. He's in the city now visiting his parents. Heard it on the radio."

"Done," said Monty, sweeping the sheet out from under Wayne's chin so that the hairs on it floated neatly to the floor like snowfall in a glass bubble. Monty twirled the sheet like a toreador and laid it neatly in one movement on the empty barber chair next to him. It was Monty's trademark. That little move. Been doing it for thirty-six years.

Wayne got out of the chair. He always gave Monty a dollar tip. Wayne always said, "Thank you kindly, Mr. Czerbiak, sir."

He did this time, too. Photopopolus had put down the magazine and was walking slowly, stoop-shouldered toward the chair. He looked like a gnome with a secret. Photopopolus had perfected the knowing look to hide his basic lack of intelligence.

"You got a gun?" Monty asked Wayne, wrapping the cloth

around Photopopolus's wrinkled neck. "You going to shoot someone, you need a gun. Am I right or am I right?"

"Yeah," said Wayne. "I've got a gun."

Wayne went out the door and onto the sidewalk in front of the mall shops. The gun in his pocket belonged to his father. Kept it loaded in a drawer in the shop. Until today.

The young man, whose name was David Sen, was certainly feeling the pain of the tightly knotted cord that bound his hands together behind the chair in which he was sitting.

Parker Liao sat about five feet away facing the young man. He was sitting in a straight-backed chair just like David Sen's, but Parker's hands were not tied.

It was a game. Both men knew it and both knew who the winner would be.

"He's alive," said Parker Liao, folding one leg over the other and clasping his hands.

David Sen didn't even consider pleading. He tried to keep his voice steady as he said, "I only got one shot. They, his people, came running in. I was lucky to get away."

"*Lucky* is a relative term," said Parker. "Because you got away you are here. Are you feeling lucky?"

Both men were in their mid-twenties. Both had been born in Chicago. Both were Chinese and members of the Twin Dragons. There were thirty-eight Twin Dragons.

Parker was the leader, a responsibility he took seriously. The latest clash with Los Tentaculos had not been about turf but about pride. Mr. Woo, who oversaw the criminal enterprises of Chinatown, had given the Dragons an assignment. He had no gang, just five bodyguards. Were he to need evidence of his control, he could have several hundred men from both the United States and Canada standing next to him within a day.

Mr. Woo cultivated a mystique drawn from Old World myths and American-breed images. He often wore silk Chinese robes when he held an audience. He burned incense, an odor that irritated him, when he wanted to impress a visitor or enemy. He had begun as a thief in Shanghai sixty years ago and bribed, stole, and murdered his way to respectability. He had come to America and learned that playing to a stereotype had advantages in dealing both with white Americans and with Chinese. Gradually, very gradually over the course of decades, Mr. Woo had grown accustomed to and comfortable with the persona he had created. He had become what at first he had only pretended to be. He was well aware of this and accepted it with no discomfort.

Mr. Woo had sent Parker to convince the policeman named Hanrahan not to marry Iris Chen. Mr. Woo had wanted to marry Iris Chen. It had been an honor to bestow on her rather than a command. He had failed. Woo had graciously accepted defeat, but Parker Liao did not accept defeat with dignity.

Not that Parker was really into the "saving face" business, but he was very much into the power business, and the other gangs and people with whom he did business, especially Mr. Woo, assumed that face-saving was an essential part of a Chinese gang's mantra. It was also, he knew, an essential part of the success of any gang. Parker, too, had to maintain a mystique though he really didn't give a shit about honor. He had long ago decided that life was about power and money.

When El Perro and Los Tentaculos had run him and two of his people off of North Avenue in front of several dozen watching Puerto Ricans and Mexicans, in front of Hanrahan and his partner, the old Jew, Parker knew the story would get back to Chinatown, that it would suggest weakness and a loss of both face and power, that he might have to deal with other gangs that ringed Chinatown. Blacks to the south and west. Latinos to the north. The backs of the Twin Dragons against the shore of Lake Michigan.

"I . . . ," David Sen began. "I'll take responsibility. I'll lose face."

"Face? You idiot. You'll lose more than face," Parker said, reaching down for his cup of coffee on the table in front of him. "No, maybe we should make literal what has only been figurative for thousands of years. Maybe I should have your face removed and show your corpse to the world."

Parker had no intention of mutilating the frightened would-be assassin, but he would have to do something. Failure could not be ignored.

The room was small, behind a Chinese grocery store. The smells of herbs permeated the room. Parker liked the smell. It reminded him of his mother's kitchen, of the traditional foods he liked. Parker loved history, the history of the world, particularly of China, and the history of his own family, which was not distinguished but which was comforting. He had photographs of his grandparents and great-grandparents in his apartment. The photographs had been taken in China. They all wore the garments of the ancient country. Parker had never worn anything but Western clothes. To do anything else, no matter how much he would like to make contact with his past, would look like an affectation.

On the other side of the door, waiting to find out how their leader was going to deal with Sen's failure, were three young Chinese men, the oldest twenty-four, the youngest seventeen.

"Any thoughts? Suggestions?" he asked David Sen, who sat up straight and shook his head instead of answering because his throat and tongue had suddenly gone very dry.

"Give me another chance to get him," he managed.

Parker considered the offer and said, "You'll need time to heal before you're capable of anything."

Parker drank some more coffee so that David Sen would have time to absorb what had just been said, and to wonder what it was he would have to heal from.

There was no point in arguing or pleading. David Sen could only hope. Two years ago he had graduated from Northern Illinois University with a degree in political science and a minor in Spanish language and literature. He hoped that his knowledge of Spanish was useful enough to Parker so that the punishment would not threaten his life.

He had been recruited into the Dragons because his cousin Daniel was a Dragon who had boasted about David's academic accomplishments. In truth, they had been minor and David had been unable to find a job when he graduated. It had not been all that difficult to recruit him with the promise of money for him to take care of his mother, father, and sister, and to live well himself.

But there was a price to pay. He had failed in his first true test.

Parker looked into his empty cup and put it back in the saucer. The pauses were growing longer.

"There is nothing to gain from my having you tortured or

killed," said Parker. "So I propose we give you a choice, actually any one of twenty choices."

David willed himself to stop sweating. It wasn't hot in the
room. The ceiling fan revolved, humming gently. There was
a breeze, but he felt the perspiration on his cheeks and forehead and knew that Parker saw it, too.

"Pick a finger or toe," said Parker.

David was relieved.

"The small toe on my left foot," he said.

Parker was shaking his head "no."

"Wrong choice," he said. "It lacks gravity. One more
choice and if it doesn't reflect the requirement of the situation, I'll choose."

Parker Liao rose and walked behind the seated man.
David Sen willed himself not to look back over his shoulder.
He heard the click of a folding knife being opened and then
there was a tug at his wrists and his hands were free.

"Choose," Parker said.

David thought.

And then he chose. Parker nodded his agreement and
called the three men who were waiting behind the door.

"David has made a decision," he said.

The three men looked at David Sen and then at their
leader. Parker held up the middle finger of his right hand.

"He will do it himself," said Parker.

Parker held out his hand palm up toward the three men.
The youngest stepped forward and removed a folding knife
from his pocket. He handed the knife to Parker, who opened
it and started to hand it, blade forward, to David Sen.

Sen took the knife, willing his hands not to shake. He
placed his left hand flat on the table next to Parker Liao's
empty coffee cup. He could not chop down without the risk
of mutilating one of his other fingers. He decided he would

place the point of the knife on the table next to the joint of his finger. Then, in one quick stroke, he would bring the blade down with all his strength, hoping he would not hit bone and fail to cut through.

Knife in his right hand, he flexed his fingers, locating a whorl on his knuckle. He moved the knife, readied it and was about to strike when . . .

"Wait," said Parker Liao. "I have something I want you to do before your penance."

David Sen held his breath.

For Sen it was a reprieve, not permanent, but maybe, if he redeemed himself, Parker would change his mind.

For Parker it was an opportunity to make Sen suffer and think about the moment that had almost been and would be again. Besides, the task he was about to give to David Sen might well be more frightening than cutting off one's own finger.

"Yes," said Sen, mouth dry.

"I want you to deliver a message to the Puerto Rican son of a bitch."

Marie Drewbecki was fifteen, pale, fair-skinned, pretty, and not sure whether to be frightened of the two cops or defiant. She would have chosen defiance if her friends had been watching, but they weren't and Marie's fear of the police prevailed.

They were sitting in an office at Senn High School, just her and the two beefy-looking cops, both with Irish names like you hear in television sitcoms. She had lost their names as soon as they gave them.

"Who beat you up last month, Marie?" asked Hanrahan.

She thought she heard sympathy in his voice. Maybe she was just hearing what she was hoping to hear.

"I dunno," she said with a shrug. "Just some guys. I dunno."

"They did something else to you," said O'Neil.

She turned her head away and looked at a black-and-white photograph of a Chicago subway station on the wall. It looked old. People were wearing funny clothes. She hadn't been in this office before. It belonged to the placement teacher. Marie had a long time to go before she needed placement help.

"You're a smart girl," said O'Neil. "Principal Mackie told me. Smart girl. College material."

She didn't respond, just looked at a man in the photograph. The man had a stiff collar and wore a little hat with a round top.

"There were three of them," she said without facing them.

The detectives knew this from the report of the girl's beating. There had been no descriptions of the men or their car.

"The car," O'Neil said. "Anything about it?"

"Just a car," she said. "Not too new. Not too old, you know. Just a car. I didn't get a real good look. They just screeched up on the street and piled out yelling, pushed me in the alley."

"How many doors?"

"Four? Yeah, four."

"Color?"

"I dunno. Hold it. There was something hanging from the mirror by the driver. A monkey, something. I dunno why I remember. It . . . a monkey, I think."

"They didn't use each other's names?" asked Hanrahan.

"Don't remember," she said. "Can I go back to math now?"

"Old woman died yesterday," Hanrahan said. "She was hit with a baseball bat."

Marie gulped, trying to hide it.

"She didn't bother anyone," said O'Neil. "Just an old bag lady. Whoever did it just wanted to have some fun. They were just having fun with you, too. Same people. Same bats they used on you. You know who they are."

"I can't," she said softly, so softly that the two detectives could barely hear her.

"What?" asked Hanrahan.

"I can't," she said a little louder and looked at him.

"They're going to hurt someone else," O'Neil said. "They killed. Next time they'll probably kill again. Maybe a girl like you. Maybe even someone you know. When you find out about it, you can remind yourself that two cops came by and asked you for help, that you could have saved her."

"Never saw them before," she said. "God's truth. Well, maybe one of them. Looked sort of like a guy works at this burger place on Irving Park. The one that has the sign in the window says, THE MOTHER OF ALL BURGERS. You know the one? Might be him, might not. Don't go asking me to identify him or anything."

"What's he look like, this guy?"

"I dunno," she said, squirming slightly. "Just a guy, maybe twenty, maybe not. Got one of those little tiny beards under his lip. Right here."

She pointed to the spot.

"It's called a goatee," Hanrahan said.

"Whatever," she said nervously.

"Where on Irving Park?" Hanrahan went on.

"Berg's," she said. "Right near Crawford. Jew place. You find him, you won't tell him I said?"

"No," said Hanrahan, getting up.

"Can I please go back to math now?"

"Sure," Hanrahan said.

She got out of the chair and hurried out of the office leaving the door open.

"Feel like a burger?" said Hanrahan.

"Maybe the mother of all burgers with cheese," answered O'Neil.

The list of people who might have wanted Connie Gower dead was long, and that was just the people Lieberman knew about, people for whom Connie had committed murder.

Lieberman pushed the white button next to the door of 3432 Indian Burial Ground Road. The neighborhood was filled with tiny adobe houses on small lots. The houses had once been coral, pink, and yellow, but time and neglect had left only the hint of original color. The small front yard to the right of where he stood was neatly kept and covered with cracking stone or concrete. The house on the left was strewn with shirtless, laughing children and two torn aluminum and plastic lawn chairs.

The building in front of which Lieberman stood pressing the white button was out of place, a three-story wooden box recently painted blood red.

The sun was just going down.

After seeing Billy Johnstone, Lieberman had gone to the downtown Yuma police station, where he found Martin Parsons at a desk in the corner of a room. There were three other desks, all empty.

Parsons had raised his eyes from the computer screen, fingers lightly touching the keys.

"How's he look?" Parsons had asked.

"Skinny, weak," said Lieberman, taking a seat next to the desk.

"Just checked with the hospital. Touch and go. But it looks like he'll make it."

"You all right?" asked Lieberman.

"Never shot anyone before. Doesn't feel real. I had to shoot him didn't I? I mean, it was righteous, right?"

"Absolutely," said Lieberman. "Probably saved my life, maybe yours too."

"You in trouble?" asked Parsons. "I mean back in Chicago."

"I lost a prisoner," said Lieberman. "My boss isn't happy, but I explained."

"He a hard-ass?"

"Can be," said Abe. "Not usually. What do you have on Johnstone?"

Parsons picked up a spiral-topped notebook, flipped it open and scanned his penciled notes.

"No record. Worked at the airport for the last sixteen years plus. Wife died eight years ago. Active member of the Liberty Baptist Church of Arizona. Lives alone on Indian Burial Ground Road. Apartment."

Parsons wrote the address on a sheet of paper and handed it to Lieberman, who tucked it in his pocket and asked, "You coming?"

Parsons shook his head "no."

"Want to finish this report," he said, pointing to the computer screen. "You ever shot anyone?"

"A few," said Lieberman.

Parsons looked as if he were going to say something, changed his mind and shook it off.

Before leaving the station Lieberman had called home. His ten-year-old granddaughter Melissa had answered.

"Grandma's out," the girl said. "Went to the grocery. She's picking up a cooked chicken and mint-chocolate ice cream and a salad."

"And two hard-boiled eggs," Lieberman added.

"Marx Brothers," she said with a giggle.

"Make that three hard-boiled eggs."

"Grandpa," Melissa pleaded. "Be serious."

"I'm always serious. Make that four hard-boiled eggs. Where's Barry?"

"Dining room, going over his speech again. If you ask me, I'd say he knows it too well. It won't make any sense to him. He'll know it so well, he'll just forget it when he's up there on the *bimah*."

"You tell him that?"

"No, never."

"Good. Tell your grandma I'll call later tonight or in the morning."

"You're in Arizona?"

"Yuma."

"Is it hot?"

"No."

"Good. Gotta go."

She hung up.

Abe pushed the button by the door of the red building again. Hard, long. He thought he heard someone inside.

The door opened. A lean, very dark, pretty black woman with her hair pulled back tightly looked at him while she adjusted an earring in her right ear. She was wearing a dark, snug-fitting dress and a pearl necklace. Door open she looked at him.

"You a cop?" she asked.

"Yeah. Want to see my shield?"

"I've seen plenty," she said. "You look kind of old to be a cop."

"I'm a Chicago cop. We grow old on the job. What made you think I was a cop?"

The children next door whooped and screamed. The

woman in front of him stood on the threshold adjusting the earring.

"News, television. Billy Johnstone's on every channel."

"You've got nice earlobes," he said.

"Earlobes?"

"My daughter has nice earlobes and a bad disposition," he said.

"Sounds like me."

"You the owner?"

"Of this mansion?" she asked, looking around with a smile. "Yes, I'm the owner."

"I like the color," Abe said.

"Stands out, doesn't it?"

"Can I come in?"

"I'm in a hurry," she said. "Got a date with a real estate man."

"I'm happy to hear it. We can talk here."

"About Billy?"

"Unless you have something else you want to talk about."

She shrugged, checked her watch, and folded her arms impatiently.

"Miss . . . ?"

"Mrs. Alvarado, Jean Alvarado."

"*Bueno,*" said Lieberman. "*Habla español? Si usted se habla, tengo mucho gusto a hacerle.*"

"I speak a hell of a lot better Spanish than you do," she said. "But why the hell would I want to? Senor Alvarado, the bruised banana from Nicaragua, left here four years ago and took all my need for Spanish with him. So stick with English. Can we . . . ?"

"Billy Johnstone. He have any friends?"

"Some, nobody close. Grandkids come and visit him now and again."

"What does he do with his time?"

"Stays in his apartment. Watches television, sometimes too loud. Turns it down when reminded. Has his meals at the airport or in his apartment. One or two nights a week he spends a few hours over at the Cantina Azul Pub. You come from downtown?"

"Yes."

"Then you must have passed it. Anything else?"

She checked her watch again.

"Two questions. First, what do you think of Billy Johnstone?"

"Think about him? Lord God and Jesus save me, I hardly think about him at all. He never causes trouble. Minds his business. Pays his rent on time. Damn. Didn't think of that. I guess he won't be coming back here. I'll have to put up the sign. You said you had two questions."

"Right," said Lieberman. "Can I take a look at Mr. Johnstone's apartment? It won't take me long."

"Damn right it won't take long. We're only talking about one room and what is optimistically called a kitchenette. Sure, but make it quick. I gotta go."

She stepped back to let Abe in.

"I owe you one, Mrs. A.," he said.

"Hell, you owe me two. Car parked across the street," she said without looking in that direction. "Been watching us. Backup in case I come out with guns in both hands blazing away?"

"No."

"Then someone's watching your very vulnerable skinny white behind."

Lieberman did not look back. He stepped further into the small seven-by-seven lobby of the building as she closed the door. Then he turned and went to the curtained window to the left of the door. He pulled the curtain back slightly and looked across the street at the tan Mazda. The person behind the wheel was a man wearing dark glasses and a cap. He was looking at the apartment door.

"Use your phone?"

"Local call?"

"Local call."

She led him through an open door and pointed to a phone on a table across the small living room. The deco room looked as if it came out of an Astaire-Rogers movie. Lieberman checked his notebook and called Parsons.

"That address you gave me. I'm inside the building. There's a tan Mazda across the street watching. Can you pick him up?"

"I'll have a car there in about ten minutes."

"It'll take that long to check out Johnstone's apartment."

Abe hung up and found himself facing the woman.

"I shouldn't have told you about that car. Now I've got to wait till the troops arrive."

"No, just let me into the apartment and make your date. I promise I won't steal anything."

"You know how many promises I've heard from men in my life both as an adult and a child?"

"Four hundred and six," said Lieberman.

"Forget it. Come on."

She led the way to the narrow steps in the little lobby and started up.

After she opened the door to the studio apartment, she stood back and said, "I'm late. You're on your own. From now on you'll have to make it through life without me."

"John Huston said that in *The Treasure of the Sierra Madre*," Abe said, looking around the room.

"I know," she said, looking at her watch. "I watch a lot of late-night TV."

"Me, too. Insomnia."

"I don't even have that excuse," she said. "Close the door when you leave."

She left and as Lieberman heard her going down the stairs, he closed the door and moved to the window. He could see the Mazda parked across the street, a figure inside it.

The room had a dark wooden floor with a faded throw rug that might or might not be Indian, American Indian. The faded gray wall on the left was covered with photographs of smiling, eyes-alive black children, a boy and a girl. From left to right along the wall the children grew older, lost and gained teeth and glasses, and a knowing depth to their smiles.

There was also a framed sheet from a ballpark souvenir book. It was a color photo of fifteen baseball players in blue uniforms. An infinitely younger and happier-looking Billy Johnstone knelt on one end of the first row.

On the wall facing this one was a gallery of black-and-white photographs, about thirty of them. All were neatly and simply framed. About half were of people, all kinds of people, all ages, colors, sizes, and locations. The other half were brooding objects, rocks, trees, storefronts, a fire hydrant with its paint cracking.

There wasn't much to search. One bleached-out yellow flowered sofa with nothing under or behind the pillows; one rocking chair, three kitchenette cabinets; an old humming refrigerator; a small chest of drawers with socks and underwear neatly laid out; and a closet as neat as the drawers with five shirts, a few pair of slacks, and a surprise on the shelf. The surprise was in a cardboard box with a red rubber band around it. Johnstone had made no attempt to hide it.

Lieberman opened the box and found more family photographs, some old letters paper-clipped together, and a full-color photograph of a white man's hand. The cuff of a shirt buttoned at the wrist was nothing special, but the man's hand was. The thumbnail was black, not the flat black of a recent hammer, but a rough gnarled ridge.

He pocketed the photograph and put the box back on the shelf. Back at the window he looked out to see a marked squad car parked behind the Mazda. Two uniformed officers were standing next to a man who was fishing something, probably his driver's license, from his wallet.

The man was tall, white-haired, ponytail, not much of a chin. He was wearing jeans and a purple T-shirt. He glanced up at the window, saw Lieberman, smiled and gave a little flip-off wave before returning his attention to the cops.

Lieberman was feeling hungry. The white-haired man would have to wait.

He was heading for the door when the phone rang. Lieberman saw the phone on the wall in the kitchen area. He moved to it, picked it up and said, "Yeah."

"Detective Lieberman, do you know where you are?"

"Generally? Specifically?"

"You are out of your element, out of your city, out of your jurisdiction, and you know where I am?"

"Out of your mind," Lieberman said dryly.

The man laughed.

"Heard about your sense of humor."

"Maybe I should be a stand-up comic."

"Pay's bad, hours are bad, and audiences are brutal," said the man.

"Thanks," said Abe. "We just going to keep chatting or do you have something to say?"

"Go home," the man said. "You've got a lovely wife, a troubled daughter, two terrific grandchildren. Go home."

"Those things I know," said Lieberman. "Tell me something I don't know."

"You're wasting your time. Johnstone's not going to talk to you. And what do you really, down deep, care if Connie Gower is dead?"

Lieberman tucked the phone under his chin and reached over to pull one of the two white kitchen chairs in the tiny alcove. He sat as he spoke.

"He was my responsibility. And I take umbrage at someone shooting people I'm handcuffed to."

"It's been nice talking to you," the man said. "No, really it's been nice."

"Thanks. I've been told I'm a sardonic conversationalist."

"That you are," said the man. "Go home."

"Soon," Lieberman said.

"Keep your Jew nose out of this," the man said.

"And you keep your thumb in your mouth."

The man hung up.

Conclusion, thought Lieberman. There's something to learn in Yuma.

O'Neil took a bite of his Big Berg Burger and scooted back to keep mustard from dripping on his shoes. He was standing next to Hanrahan at a little round wood-colored plastic table. Hanrahan had taken a bite of the hot dog in front of him. The table was dappled with poppy seeds from the bun.

Two men in their thirties with grease on their hands, faces, and T-shirts were carrying on a mouthful conversation about the Bears' chances at a play-off spot next season.

There were two people with white aprons behind the

counter. One was a heavy man about forty-five with a head of dark hair. He kept wiping his hands on the stained apron. The other person behind the counter was a skinny woman wearing too much makeup. Both cops sized her up as being somewhere between sixty-five and eternity.

"Stuff's good," said O'Neil. "Never been in here before."

"Come and go," said Hanrahan.

"Huh?"

"Places around here come and go."

Hanrahan took out his wallet, nodded at the heavy guy in the apron who was looking at them, and showed his shield. He nodded for the man to come over.

The heavy guy nodded, glanced at the door, said something to the old woman, wiped his hands, and disappeared to his right. He came out through a door near the restroom looking uncomfortable.

"Something wrong?" he asked.

"You Berg?" asked O'Neil.

"Yes," he said. "Bert Berg."

"Good burger."

"Top ground round," said Berg. "What can I do for you?"

"Kid around eighteen or nineteen. Goatee," said Hanrahan, pointing to his own face to indicate where the goatee would be. "Drives a dark car with a monkey on the dash."

"Yeah?" the man said, wiping his hands again.

"Know him?" asked O'Neil, taking another bite.

"Don't think so."

Berg glanced quickly at the woman on the other side of the counter, who was straining to hear what was being said.

"Think harder," O'Neil said, chancing a large bite of his sandwich.

"I don't know," Berg said with a shrug. "I mean we've got

people in and out, regulars, not regulars. Doesn't ring a bell. What did he do?"

"Something bad," said O'Neil.

"Like . . . ?"

"Something bad," O'Neil repeated. "Who works behind the counter?"

"Me, my mother."

"No one else?" asked Hanrahan.

"My son sometimes."

"Where is he?" asked O'Neil.

Berg looked at his mother and then back at the policemen.

"Out. He doesn't work today. Why?"

"We want to talk to him," said O'Neil.

Hanrahan fished into his pocket and came up with a card slightly bent at the corner. He handed it to Berg, who wiped his hands again before taking it with a nod.

O'Neil had finished his burger and was cleaning his fingers with a napkin. Hanrahan picked up his half-eaten hot dog.

"We'll be back," said O'Neil, dropping his crumpled napkin on the table.

"But . . . ," Berg began.

"Good burgers," O'Neil explained.

The arguing men at the other table paused in their conversation. One of them stepped in front of the two detectives, who were heading for the door.

"You're what's-his-name," said the young man pointing a grimy finger at Hanrahan. "Played on the line back with McMahon. Seventies. Right?"

"No," said Hanrahan.

"You look like him," said the other man. "You're sure you're not him?"

"I'm Dick Butkus," said O'Neil.

"Like hell," said the first man at the table.

"I've had plastic surgery," O'Neil insisted.

"Like hell," the man repeated.

The two cops moved through the door and out onto the sidewalk.

"Berg recognized the description," O'Neil said.

"He recognized," said Hanrahan.

"It's his kid," said O'Neil.

"It is."

"Stakeout?"

"They'll probably call him, tell him we're looking for him," said Hanrahan.

They both looked back through the window where Berg couldn't help looking at them for an instant from behind the counter. An old man with a Cubs cap and a walker accompanied by a younger woman with a coat and scarf moved into the store.

"Give him a few hours and come back?" asked O'Neil.

"Yeah, let him think," said Hanrahan.

"About junior's dirty hands," said O'Neil.

They walked down the sidewalk and got into their car.

Inside the store, the woman in the apron whispered, "I heard, Bert."

Berg turned to look at the man with the walker who moved slowly toward him.

"Ma, forget it."

"They'll come back," she said.

"And I still won't know anything. Ma, let it be."

"Paul did something wrong, Bert, something very wrong."

Berg wiped his hands and said to the man with the walker, "Mr. G.G., the usual?"

Wayne considered whistling. He was a good whistler, whistled right along with songs on the oldies radio station while he worked. He could warble, trill, and keep up with any tune. "Heartaches," "Yesterdays," "Bad Moon Rising," "Hard Drinking Woman." Wayne decided it wasn't the right thing to do.

Lee Cole Carter was visiting his father and mother. He came back when he was in the area doing a show. He brought them something they didn't need or want and gave them tickets to his show they wouldn't use. Lee Cole's mother and father always acted pleased to get the modern-looking lamp or new television to replace their new television. Lee Cole never stayed long, an hour or two at the most. He was always in a hurry, had someplace to go. Lee Cole's mother had come to expect this. She would always have coffee and some butter cookies ready. Sometimes he would drink a half-cup of coffee and eat a cookie or two before looking at his gold Rolex.

"Go, Lee," she would say. "I know you're busy. We're proud of you."

"Very proud," Lee Cole's father Gregory would say with a smile he didn't mean, happy that his son, who had dyed his hair and wore an earring and a cowboy hat, would be out of his life till the next visit. Gregory was a cop, retired. He couldn't carry a tune. Neither could his wife, and Gregory didn't think their son Lee Cole did an awful goddamn good job of it either. Besides, Gregory could tell from his breath that Lee Cole had been smoking. The smell was also on his son's clothes. He was glad when Lee Cole, named for his mother's father, was gone, back on the television and the radio and the tapes where he could be turned off.

It was toward the apartment of Mr. and Mrs. Gregory Carter that Wayne, clean-shaven, hair freshly cut, determined look on his face, headed. He wanted to look his very best for the photographers. He was about to earn respect and recognition. People would remember the man who killed Lee Cole Carter. Some country-and-western song might even be written about him. George Strait would be the one who should sing it. Or maybe Faith Hill.

He walked. He could have taken his car. He had a 1997 GEO Prizm. It was blue. He kept it in good condition, but didn't have much of anywhere to drive it.

He didn't need his car. Not today. He was going to shoot Lee Cole Carter with the gun in his pocket and then wait for the police. There might be someone with Lee Cole. He would shoot him or her or them, too. He might have to shoot Lee Cole three or four or more times. There were enough bullets in the gun. He wanted to be sure. He didn't want to be the man who tried to kill the sort-of-famous Lee Cole Carter. He wanted to be the man who killed the celebrity.

Emiliano "El Perro" Del Sol, which was not his real name, had never personally killed anyone in a hospital. Two of his men had thrown someone off of a hospital roof a little over a year ago, but that had been a favor for Lieberman, *El Viejo*.

However, El Perro was now considering murder in a hospital. His room was private. Piedras, he of great strength and little mind, stood guarding the door, hands at his side, ready to do whatever El Perro ordered.

El Perro considered.

Piedras could silently kill both of the Chinese men in dark suits who stood next to the bed. Getting rid of their bodies would be as easy as opening the window and throwing them out. That could be done while they were alive, but since it was only the fourth floor, El Perro would want to be sure they didn't survive. Besides, he thought as he fingered the white scar on his face, true satisfaction could come only if El Perro did the killing himself. But, why not?

David Sen looked down at the mad Puerto Rican, hoping that he appeared cool and inscrutable. At his side was Victor Tung, short, muscled, expendable. David knew he, too, was expendable.

"So?" asked El Perro, hands under the blanket. He was propped up and waiting impatiently.

"The Twin Dragons will accept your apology," Sen said. "You must do so publicly, on Wednesday night."

On Wednesday nights—and Saturdays, too—El Perro called the bingo numbers at the hall he owned on North Avenue. He called numbers with a wild abandon that was known throughout the Hispanic community. He had names for each number, each ball.

"Alive, alive, before B-five," he would shout, holding up a white ball as if it were a trophy eyeball.

"You're the one who shot me," said El Perro.

"Me? No. We all look pretty much alike, don't we?"

"Not to me," said El Perro.

"Well?" asked Sen, fighting the urge to escape those mad brown eyes looking at him.

"I have a message for Liao," El Perro said. "But you can't deliver it. The message is he can get on his hands and knees and I'll drop my pants so he can do me. Then he can have the choice of killing himself with a knife or me killing him with a baseball bat."

Sen said nothing. Victor Tung said nothing.

"You want me to deliver that message?" asked Sen.

"No," said El Perro. "Your friend there. You're dead."

El Perro's left hand came out from under the blanket, a gun with a silencer. He fired as Piedras moved forward to put an arm around the neck of Victor Tung.

The first of two fired bullets crushed the bridge of David Sen's nose. He stood, mouth open, and the second bullet ripped through his tongue and the back of his head. Sen crumpled forward, hitting his head on the metallic foot of the bed as he dropped to the floor. He was most certainly dead.

Piedras relieved Tung of the gun under his leather jacket.

"Piedras, *la ventana*," El Perro said, gun aimed at Tung.

Piedras nodded and moved to the window. It was already opened a crack. He finished, gently pushed out the screen, pulled the screen in, lifted the window, and turned to the bed.

"How much blood?" El Perro asked.

Piedras examined the floor.

"No hay mucho," he said.

"Clean it up fast."

Tung watched, left hand twitching uncontrollably. Piedras

went to the bathroom, got paper towels, and cleaned up quickly. When he was done, he turned to his leader, who said,

"*Ahora.*"

Piedras picked up the body like a bouncer in an old movie, one hand on the seat of his pants, the other on his collar. He heaved the dead man out the window, quickly replaced the screen, closed and locked the window, and moved to the bed. El Perro handed him the gun. He tucked the gun in his belt and pulled out his shirt so it would cover the weapon.

"Give Liao the message," El Perro said to Tung as Piedras went to the door and opened it.

"What message?" asked Tung.

"What message? The one you just saw, you fucking stupid Chink."

"'Faubus,' you ever hear that name?" asked Lieberman, sitting next to the bed.

There was a rumbling outside the hospital. Sounded like thunder.

"Garbage pickup," said Billy Johnstone. "I know the sound of garbage pickup."

He still looked terrible, but terrible was better than hopeless.

"You a garbage pro?"

"That I am," said Johnstone with what might have been a smile. There was a catch in his throat as if he needed to get something reluctant down and out of the way. "Been lots of things, but right fielder and janitor are what I've known best."

Lieberman nodded and said, "Janitor? Not sanitary engineer?"

"Hell no," Johnstone said, trying to keep his fluttering

eyes focused. "Indians are Indians, not Native Americans. Chinese are Oriental."

"And Asian."

"And Asian," Johnstone agreed.

"And people like me are Negroes or Blacks, not African-American. Why should all of us minorities keep changing our names?"

"Keeps white people off-guard," said Lieberman.

"Maybe."

Silence in the small room. Garbage bins kept rattling.

"Faubus," said Lieberman again. "About six-two, forty years old, white hair tied back."

Billy Johnstone shook his head, but slowly and just a little. "James Faubus, Cowboy Faubus?"

"In Yuma about half the white people call themselves Cowboy this or that," said Johnstone. "Closest all of them ever came to a cow was when it was medium rare and on a plate. There was a Faubus, governor of Mississippi, Louisiana, someplace like that back when I was in Triple A back in the fifties."

"Arkansas," said Lieberman.

"Threw Negroes out of diners or kept them from going to college or something."

"High school," said Lieberman. "Little Rock."

"Right," said Billy. "Now I'm remembering. This Cowboy of yours some relation to him? The governor of Arkansas?"

The garbage truck was grinding away now. Lieberman paused to wait till it was finished digesting.

"That was Orville Faubus. I don't know if the gentleman I talked to an hour ago was related. You never know. I do know he was following me. Want to know why?"

Billy didn't answer.

"Cowboy Faubus has a record. Nothing big. Black market cigarettes. Attempted extortion."

"He steal a horse?" asked Billy hoarsely. "That's a hanging deal in the West. Saw it on *Bonanza* way back."

"You're amused," said Lieberman.

"Just getting tired," said Billy softly.

"I'm coming to the good part," said Lieberman. "I'll give you the short version. Faubus says a man paid him five hundred dollars to follow me and report to him. Man didn't give him a name or number. Man said he'd check in from time to time."

Billy said nothing.

"The Cowboy described the man," Lieberman continued, crossing his legs, feeling the ache of sitting in one position for too long. "Pretty ordinary. White. Five-eight maybe. Fifty years old maybe. Average weight maybe. Face that looks like everybody else."

"You believe him? I mean that he can describe this fella?" Billy said.

"Yes, because of one detail. The thumb on the man's left hand."

Billy's eyes popped open, suddenly alert.

Lieberman had the photo he had taken from Billy's apartment in his hand. He held it up so the man in the bed could see.

"How'd you get the picture?"

Billy pursed his lips and his head nodded forward and back as if a song were running through his memory. Then he spoke.

"Had the camera in my hand. Taking pictures at the river. He came up to me. Knew all about me. Made the proposition."

"To kill Gower and get your grandchildren's college education paid for."

"Not saying yes and not saying no here."

The garbage truck rumbled away slowly, hitting bumps in the street, playing trash music for the masses and the sick and dying.

"He didn't know you took the picture."

"Didn't have a hint," said Billy.

"Too good an ID to pass up," said Lieberman.

"Maybe something like that. Wasn't thinking too much at the time. Crazy proposition comes out of who knows where by this guy. I see his messed-up thumbnail, got the camera in my hand. What the hell."

"What the hell," Lieberman agreed. "Did he pay you everything he promised or was there going to be a payment after you killed Gower?"

"Paid up-front," said Billy. "Made it clear if I didn't do it, he'd want his money back or my grandkids dead. That's the part he shouldn't have said. Money's already in a trust for them. You can't get it. He can't get it. And if you say I got it, it's your word against mine and I can call you a liar with the emotion of a weeping old man if it comes to that."

"I don't want to get at your grandkids' money. I want the guy with the bad thumbnail. Give me something I can work with."

Billy was looking at the ceiling now. He looked at the ceiling so long that Lieberman considered looking up there to see what was so interesting, but he didn't. The policeman sat quietly, wondering if there was a Jewish deli in Yuma. He doubted it.

"He's not in Yuma anymore," Billy said, still looking at the ceiling.

"Where is he?"

"Don't know that but I know where he was going. Chicago."

"Chicago?"

"Answered his cell phone while we were standing there and he was conning me about how I'd be doing the world a big favor by getting rid of this Gower guy."

Billy grew silent again, looking at the ceiling.

"Cell phone," Lieberman said, bringing Billy back to the hospital room.

"He said 'meet you tomorrow at six at the place on Hoyne.' Don't know how many Hoynes there are in the U.S. but I know there's one in Chicago near Wrigley Field. Right?"

"Right."

"And the guy I killed, Gower, he's from Chicago, right?"

"Right."

"Two and two adds up for me."

It did for Lieberman, too.

"Know what Mr. Thumbnail's mistake was?" asked Billy.

"Being born?"

"No," said Billy, meeting the detective's eyes. "Threatening my grandkids."

A heavyset nurse in white with a perfect pink complexion and a round face opened the door and said apologetically, "I'm sorry. Visiting hours are over."

"You know if there's a Jewish deli in Yuma?" Lieberman asked the nurse.

She shrugged. Billy said "no."

"Then I'm going back to Chicago," Lieberman announced, standing up.

"You find him," said Billy. "If he comes back to Yuma, goes anywhere near my grandkids, I plan to send him to hell if I have to rise from the dead to do it."

Before he left, Abe would check on how many outgoing flights had gone to Chicago in the past three days. He'd get a passenger list and turn it over to Captain Kearney when he got back to the station. Abe fully expected that he would be calling a lot of recent visitors to Yuma in the next few days when he got back to Chicago. Meanwhile, he would have to decide between Tex-Mex and pizza.

The major problem for Blue Berg was finding something to do, almost anything to do that required action and not a lot of thought.

He sat behind the wheel of his car, rubbed a finger across the little beard under his lower lip, and looked through the windshield up at the moon.

Next to him in the passenger seat, Easy Dan hummed nothing softly and spun the monkey dangling from the rearview mirror.

In the backseat, Comedy, that was all, just Comedy, leaned back with his eyes closed, hands folded, thumbs twitching. He had a name but no one used it.

They were waiting for Blue to decide what they were going to do tonight. They had to do something. None of them could sit through a movie, a ball game, the first five words of a book or even more than a short paragraph in *People* magazine. Music? If it pounded and they didn't have to pay attention.

Easy Dan and Comedy moved to Blue Berg's music, the thumping heels of his hands against the steering wheel, his nodding head while he decided what they were going to do. Only when they did whatever Blue told them to do did they begin to feel the rush. Wound tight, tight, tighter, Blue would drive, scanning the streets, palms pounding the steering wheel to the beat of something on the radio. Comedy and Easy Dan would scan, too, but they relied on Blue to make the decision.

And when he did, it was like fucking magic. There were a couple of spic girls, or a woman and kid, or an old bag lady. He didn't have to tell them what to do. They heard the trunk pop open, got out, pulled the bats and felt their blood going nuts inside them.

Then, when it was over, and they could feel their blood rumble-rambling like a runaway El train underground, they would turn the radio on, high, something that sounded like aluminum bats on a drum, that their hearts could keep time with, racing along with a squealing electric guitar.

Blue's name wasn't Blue. It was Paul.

Easy Dan's real name was Daniel Rostinski.

Comedy had been born and christened and stuck George Grosse.

Together they called themselves the Blue Glee Club. The name had been Comedy's idea. He had funny ideas like that.

Blue started the car and shot into traffic on Western Avenue, almost hitting a white pickup truck. The pickup's driver swerved, almost hitting a yellow subcompact in the next lane.

The pickup driver sped up as Blue stepped on the gas. The pickup came alongside Blue's car. Blue smiled. The pickup's driver was a man wearing a baseball cap. He needed major dental work. A cigar was clenched in his teeth. He glared down at Blue, who kept smiling. The pickup hit his horn — beep, beep . . . beep, beep. Blue looked over at the man, who gave Blue the finger.

Traffic wasn't heavy, but there was traffic.

Blue reached under his seat and came up with a pistol. He rolled down the window, looked at the guy in the pickup, showed the weapon.

The guy in the pickup spat his cigar on the floor, hit his horn again, and shouted something.

Blue fired.

"Holy shit," Comedy shouted and laughed.

The passenger window of the pickup was down. The bullet went through the windshield, shattering glass.

"Cold Blue. Ice Blue. Cold Blue," said Easy Dan watching as the pickup lost control, shot further into traffic. Comedy turned to watch it through the rear window. The pickup was facing the other way now. A passing blue Buick clipped the left fender of the pickup and spun it back into an about-face.

Blue drove.

"Good fucking start," said Comedy. "What now?"

"Cruise mode," said Blue. He had an idea of where he was heading but he didn't want to turn it into a decision. He wanted it to pop open and be there.

Blue put the gun back under the seat and drove.

Hanrahan parked in front his house on Ravenswood, the house he and Maureen had bought when he became a cop, the house in which they had raised two boys, the house Maureen had walked away from when Bill had failed for about the sixth time to conquer the bottle. It had been hard for Maureen. She had been a good Catholic. Bill knew she no longer considered herself a good Catholic. She had traded a lifetime of piety for relative peace of mind and she was content with the trade. Bill didn't blame her.

Keys in hand, he walked up the short walkway to the three steps, stood in front of the door and inserted his key.

Bill was sober, remarried. He had waited three years for Maureen to come back. He had kept the house glossy clean though he was seldom there except to sleep. Maureen had made a new life. Bill had kept the house clean. New vacuum cleaner, Pine-Sol, Windex, Swiffer, mops, oven cleaner. But Maureen had made a new life. Eventually, so did Bill.

"Bill?" Iris called as he stepped in.

"William Patrick Hanrahan, the hobbled Irish bear of song and legend," he said.

Iris was out of the chair and moving toward him with a smile. Bill wondered where Iris, who was almost fifty, got the smooth skin, the perfect body. Not from her father, the wizened Chinese twig. Iris's mother had died when Iris was a child. There were no photographs of her.

Bill took her in his arms and kissed her, a soft, gentle kiss. She pulled her head back to look at him. Her eyes were brown and deep and moist.

"You're on time," she said.

"On time," he agreed.

"Wonders never cease," she said. "Hungry?"

"Hungry," he said.

"Good. So am I. We either sit in the kitchen while I put something together or we go out."

"You working tonight?"

"Two hours. I'll close," she said.

Iris had worked full-time in her father's small Chinese restaurant on Sheridan Road just south of Devon. The restaurant was in a motel. Now she filled in afternoons and a few nights. The rest of the time one of her younger sisters, Vicki, waited tables.

"Meaning you want to go out," he said.

"Yes."

"Greek."

"Yes."

Iris was a sucker for gyros.

"Let's do it."

"I need a sweater?"

"Wouldn't hurt to bring one."

She grabbed a white sweater from the rack next to the door.

Hanrahan opened the door and found himself facing Sean O'Neil, who was reaching for the door knocker.

"Your cell's not on," O'Neil said, looking at Iris in a way Hanrahan definitely did not care for. It wasn't quite a leer, but when his eyes met Bill's, Hanrahan sensed the unspoken words, "Nice piece of Chinese ass you picked up."

"I know," said Bill.

"Got a call a few minutes after you took off," said O'Neil. "Nurse at Swedish Covenant raped, beaten. Our boys' MO. Like a signed piece of work. Mrs. Hanrahan, I'm your husband's partner, Sean O'Neil."

"Temporary partner," said Hanrahan.

Iris nodded.

"Where is she?"

"In the hospital. Covenant. They jumped her in the parking lot. She crawled about fifty feet to the emergency room door."

Bill looked at Iris with an unspoken apology.

"It's all right," she said. "I'll go help my father for an extra hour or two."

"Good meeting you, Mrs. H," said O'Neil.

Iris said nothing. Bill gave her a quick kiss and followed O'Neil out the door.

"Your car or mine?" O'Neil asked.

"Mine," said Hanrahan. "I'll drive you back here later."

They got into Bill's car and O'Neil, who seemed to be in a particularly good mood, said, "Nice woman, your wife."

Bill drove slowly. One word out of line, one hint and he

knew he would throw an elbow into O'Neil's stomach. In one motion, Bill would throw the elbow, stop the car, reach over and open the door, and push O'Neil over while holding his shoulder so O'Neil could throw up if he had to.

O'Neil said nothing as they drove down Wilson. The hospital was on Foster near Kedzie. One of Lieberman's favorite hot dog stands was right near Swedish Covenant.

"I live alone," O'Neil finally said, looking out the window at the night neon.

Hanrahan said nothing.

"Wife died. Big C. No kids. No family."

"Sorry," said Hanrahan.

"Landa Carrier. Remember her?"

The name was . . . "Records clerk downtown?"

"That's the one," said O'Neil.

Landa Carrier was black.

"I didn't know," said Hanrahan.

"That she was dead or that she married me?"

"Both."

"Then how come . . . ?"

"Nothing's simple, William," said O'Neil. "She was the exception. There are always exceptions. Some screwing up of souls or something. She should have been born white. Her father was a black son of a bitch. Her mother . . . so fucking cold you could chip chunks off of her with a hammer. Your wife looks like an exception."

"My wife looks Chinese. Hungry?"

O'Neil grinned.

"Guess I am."

"I know a hot dog place near the hospital."

"I'm feeling generous, partner," said O'Neil. "Warm poppy seed buns? Koshers?"

Hanrahan nodded.

"Dogs are on me," said O'Neil. "I'm in a good mood."

Hanrahan stepped on the gas and prayed to the Virgin Mother and St. Joseph to get Lieberman back to Chicago before he lost his job and pension for killing a fellow officer.

He walked. Nice sunny day. Slight breeze. Crows cawing somewhere but he couldn't see them. The streets were almost empty. He was just turning into the driveway of the Fair Breeze Condos on Sheridan. A lady came out of the doorway putting on white gloves as she walked toward him with a smile. She was a friend of Wayne's mother. Her name was Stella Armstrong.

"Wayne," she said.

"Mrs. Armstrong."

"You visiting someone?"

"No," he said. "I'm here to shoot Lee Cole Carter."

Mrs. Armstrong thought Wayne meant he was going to take the singer's photograph. He wasn't carrying a camera, but they were so small nowadays that you could carry one in your pocket. Wayne was a painter, not a photographer, but maybe, Mrs. Armstrong thought, he took photographs and then went back and painted pictures from them, not that she recalled any real paintings of people Wayne had ever done.

"Got to get to an appointment with my doctor," she said apologetically. "I've got a thing on my back. Down here, you see?"

Wayne nodded and smiled at her as she passed him. She smelled like lilacs.

It was almost midnight when Abe pulled into the garage behind his house in West Rogers Park. Getting home felt good, right, comfortable.

Abe was not a born traveler. Most of the times he had left Chicago were on police business. Four of the times were trips Bess had arranged after finding out her husband's schedule.

"When you retire, we travel," Bess said about twice a year, usually with the first left hook of winter.

Lieberman didn't argue. What would be would be. He had liked Vancouver, San Diego, Mexico, and even the visit to New York for the wedding of one of Bess's cousin Devora's six sons. Devora's husband was a rabbi, ultraorthodox, complete with beard, black suit, and black hat. His name was Benjamin. Lieberman liked him even though Ben was a Mets fan.

There was a night-light outside the back door. Abe went up the two wooden steps as quietly as he could, opened the door and stepped into the kitchen, where Bess sat with a cup in her hand.

"You're back," she said with relief.

"Lieberman has returned," he said. "Not in triumph, but in the recurrent failure which is the lot of most men's lives."

"And women's, too," she said. "You hungry?"

He put down his carry-on bag and said, "Am I ever not hungry?"

Bess was wearing his favorite white nightgown. It shimmered silky as she came to him and gave him a kiss. She was a beauty. Always had been. She looked ten or more years younger than her fifty-five. He looked a good ten years older than his sixty-one. It was not uncommon for people to assume Bess was his daughter.

"You want the chicken hot or cold?" she said, moving to the refrigerator.

"Cold with Miracle Whip."

"Cold without Miracle Whip," she answered.

"Are there cholesterol police in heaven?" he asked, sitting down.

She took a platter wrapped in aluminum foil from the refrigerator and placed it on the table.

"No one has cholesterol problems in heaven," she said. "In hell everyone has cholesterol problems."

He lifted the edge of the aluminum foil and tweaked out a cold piece of brown skin.

"Avrum," Bess said with a sigh of despair, which he was sure would bring tears to the eyes of God.

"Exceptions should be made for a returning warrior," he said.

"Exceptions are for those who do not live their lives as a series of exceptions."

She handed him a plate, a knife, and a fork, poured him a glass of iced tea from the pitcher in the refrigerator, and sat while he ate.

"Tired?"

"Tired," he said, knowing that he would not be able to sleep for hours. Insomnia was one of his curses, but insomnia made him fully appreciate sleep. "What? You've got something."

"The sisters say the bar mitzvah dinner will cost eleven hundred dollars more than they thought," she said.

"Because . . . ?"

"I made the invitation list longer."

Lieberman nodded and kept eating. The chicken was good and the news was not a big surprise. He was a detective. He had expected it when he met with the two sisters who were planning the event. He looked up.

"There's more?"

"Lisa's coming."

"For the bar mitzvah," he said. "Her son's bar mitzvah. Her parents' money. When are they coming?"

"He's not coming. She is. Tomorrow."

"Her husband's not coming?"

Bess shook her head.

"How do you say *déjà vu* in Yiddish?" he asked, sneaking a small piece of skin.

"You don't," Bess said. "You just live it and expect it."

Lisa had driven away her first husband, Todd Cresswell, the father of Abe's two grandchildren. Todd, a professor of classics at Northwestern University, had remarried. Then Lisa had gone through two years of boulder-size rocky times with her present husband, Marvin Alexander, a nearly brilliant pathologist with the patience of Moses in the wilderness. Lisa had chosen him, in part, because he was black, a fact that she incorrectly assumed would be a source of pain to Lieberman. In fact, both Abe and Bess had taken to him immediately. Abe's initial thought had been "What does this man see in my daughter that I don't see?"

Lisa was pretty like her mother. That was true. Lisa was smart, a PhD in biology. But Lisa's perfectly filed mental list of complaints against her father, and by extension to all men who got too close to her, was encyclopedic.

"I'll get her at the airport," said Bess.

Lieberman nodded.

"She wants something, doesn't she?"

"She doesn't like Barry's speech."

"How about his diction?"

"Abe . . ."

He finished the last small forkful of chicken and looked at his wife.

"Dessert?"

"Fresh strawberries."

"And more *tsuris*?"

"A little."

Lieberman sat quietly. He knew that whatever it was, Bess had saved it for the last.

"Ida Katzman is dead," she said.

Mr. Woo sat at his desk and looked at the two men, Parker Liao and Victor Tung, seated across from him. Mr. Woo was well aware that his office looked like a white man's image of how a Chinese criminal lord's office should look—and not just a white man but all of the second-, third-, and fourth-generation Chinese shippers, store owners, and petty criminals who sat before him awaiting his largesse, forgiveness, or punishment.

Thin Oriental carpets, vases large and small on dark, ancient tables around the room, colorful paintings of centuries-old warriors on and off horseback, swords raised, ready. There was even a large, seated, fat and smiling Buddha alone on a table behind him. Mr. Woo, however, believed only in himself.

"And you wish my permission to start a war," said the thin and ancient Woo.

He had chosen today not to wear traditional Chinese garb, but a perfectly fitting blue suit with a tasteful blue-and-red striped tie.

"The Puerto Rican killed David Sen," said Liao. "I sent David to negotiate a peace. That lunatic shot him and threw him out a window. Victor?"

"Yes," Victor Tung said quickly.

"And this war would not be about territory or money?" Woo said.

"Honor," said Parker Liao.

"Honor," Woo repeated, looking at the frightened Victor Tung.

"Without honor there is no respect. Without respect there is no power," said Liao. "You said that."

"And if you cut off the head of the scorpion?" asked Woo.

"I tried that," said Parker. "David Sen failed."

"And he failed again at the hospital."

"Yes."

"Then it is also you who have twice failed," said Woo.

"Yes."

Woo thought for a while, looked at the two men, and said, "Do as you wish. I neither bless nor approve. I will watch and wait and in that waiting I want nothing to bring the police to Chinatown. Not a single window or vase broken or anyone who is not a Twin Dragon killed."

"I understand," said Liao.

"Go," said the old man.

Parker and Victor rose, bowed slightly, and left the room, closing the door quietly behind them.

Woo pressed a button on his desk. The door behind him next to a painting opened and a well-built Chinese in a tan suit stepped in, closing the door behind him.

"You heard?"

"Yes," said the man.

"Revenge is a disease," said Woo.

The man nodded.

"It can kill the carrier."

The man nodded again.

"At least we can hope it does. Liao is too much with us. Should he survive the war, I would like to see that he does not survive the peace which follows."

"He will not."

Hanrahan was late for the meeting at eight in the morning in Kearney's office. He knocked, entered when he heard someone's voice.

Captain Kearney was standing behind his desk at the window looking down on Clark Street. A few years ago Kearney had been the rising star in the department, honors up to his behind, second-youngest man in the history of department to make captain. Lean, darkly handsome, engaged to the daughter one of the city's biggest industrialists, Kearney was on the fast track and respected.

And then came Bernie Shepard. Bernie had been Kearney's partner. Bernie had decided that Kearney had bedded Bernie's wife, corrupting her. Bernie had shot his wife and her current lover and a few other people and holed up on a North Side roof, proclaiming to the media that his rampage was caused by Kearney.

It wasn't, but the media had picked up on it and after Shepard had been killed, still proclaiming his ex-partner's guilt, Kearney's meteoric career had ended, as had his engagement.

Kearney had aged markedly in four years and grown dark and sullen, but he was a fair man and Bill Hanrahan needed a fair man right now.

"Sorry I'm late," Bill said, looking at Sean O'Neil and Abe, who sat in the two chairs facing Kearney's desk.

O'Neil didn't turn to him. Abe did. Their eyes met and agreed that they would talk about what had happened in Yuma when they were alone.

Kearney put his hands behind his neck and worked his head from side to side before turning to face the new arrival. Kearney nodded toward the wooden table. Bill took one of the chairs and moved it next to Lieberman.

"Just found out my wife's pregnant," Hanrahan said, sitting.

Lieberman smiled and patted his partner's face with an open palm. Their eyes met again and Lieberman's were full of questions. Do you want this at your age? Is Iris too old for children? Are you all right with this? And by the way, congratulations.

"Congratulations," Kearney said flatly.

"Same," said O'Neil, without looking at Hanrahan.

And that was it. Lieberman would tell Bess. Bess would call Iris. The fussing would begin. Bill would have to tell his two grown sons. They would have to deal with it. Bill wasn't dealing at all. It was just something he had begun carrying, tucked away but real, something he would have to look at, think about later.

Kearney sighed, a small sigh, and said, "What do you have on the Connie Gower killing?"

Kearney knew that Lieberman had just gotten back the night before and had had little time to do anything. He was pushing and letting Lieberman know he would keep pushing.

"Shooter was a janitor at the Yuma airport," said Lieberman. "Hired by a guy with a disfigured right thumbnail."

Lieberman held up his right hand and tapped his thumbnail with his little finger.

"Shooter says the guy who hired him was heading to Chicago," Lieberman continued.

"You believe him?" asked Kearney.

"No reason to lie."

"Mob job?" asked Kearney.

"Could be, probably, but our Connie put away a lot of people for one reason," said Lieberman.

"Cash," said Kearney. "See the papers yesterday, today? Local news, WGN?"

If it appeared on WGN, it was national news. WGN, owned and operated by the World's Greatest Newspaper, the *Chicago Tribune*, was a cable superstation.

"No," said Lieberman.

"Let's see . . . ," Kearney began.

"Hit Man Hit," said O'Neil. "While in custody of Chicago police. Something like that."

O'Neil looked at Lieberman with false sympathy.

"Sent out an all-stations," said Lieberman. "Man with a distinctive right thumbnail. I'll check my sources."

"Find him fast. Wrap it up," said Kearney, turning to Hanrahan. "Bag lady. How hard is it to find a carful of roaming idiots with baseball bats? Very hard. Hard. Relatively hard. Easy. Impossible. Pick one."

The glance between Abe and Bill was quick, hardly perceptible. Kearney wasn't quite coming apart but he wasn't quite hanging on either.

"We've got descriptions of the car and the leader," said Hanrahan. "And a burger place on Irving Park they sometimes turn up."

"We've got them within an eight-block radius off of Irving Park and Western," said O'Neil.

"I've got some breaking news for you," said Kearney. "It'll hit television later this morning. Your merry men raped a young mother last night and broke her arm. You know who watched?"

He paused as if he actually expected an answer, his eyebrows raised.

"Her five-year-old son," said Kearney. "You know who the husband is?"

He gave them time again, knowing there would be no answering, wanting them to anticipate the worst. It came.

"Hugh Morton. Name ring a bell?"

"Detective sergeant in the Fourth," said Lieberman.

The name had also registered with Hanrahan. Morton was young, black, on the upward ladder Kearney had fallen off of. Morton held a law degree from DePaul and had won two commendations, one for talking a young Greek kid who had killed his sister into letting three hostages go, and another for arresting a deranged Gulf War vet who was planning to shoot the governor the afternoon Morton tracked him down.

Morton was a hero.

Morton was a rising star.

Morton was black. A columnist in the *Sun-Times* had called him the Colin Powell of Chicago's war against crime.

Morton's wife had been raped in front of their son.

"Shit," mumbled O'Neil.

"Your shit," Kearney said, looking at Bill and O'Neil. "And mine. Find them fast, real fast. You know why?"

"Yeah," said O'Neil.

"No," said Kearney. "You don't know why. Hugh Morton told the chief of police this morning that he plans to get the people who did this. 'Get.' That means he plans to kill them. The chief doesn't want that. I don't want it. You can understand it, but you can't want it. The public wants it. Ergo . . . ?"

"We catch the perps fast," said Bill. "Before Morton finds them."

"And you know what the problem with that is?" asked Kearney. "Morton is damned good. Morton, in fact, is better than I was. Morton is likely to get them before you do. He'll end up in jail. Then what, Abe?"

"He'll probably be elected mayor," said Lieberman.

No one laughed.

"O'Neil, you stay on the case," said Kearney. "Abe, get the man with the golden thumb. Any questions?"

Kearney didn't want any and it wouldn't have been a good idea to come up with one, but Abe did.

"I've got a funeral to go to," he said.

"When?" asked Kearney.

"In a few hours."

"Who?"

"An old woman. A friend."

"How long?"

Lieberman looked at three Irishmen. For them, he knew from Hanrahan and other Irishmen who had taken him to funerals and wakes, a funeral and its aftermath were often long hours of lamentation, celebration, and drinking.

"A few hours," said Lieberman.

Kearney shrugged.

"One more thing," said Kearney. "A Chinese kid, one of the Twin Dragons, was shot and flew, fell, or was thrown out of a window in Ravenswood Hospital. Name was David Sen. Another bell rung?"

Abe and Bill knew the name.

"One of Parker Liao's whips," said Kearney. Abe had been on the street when the Tentaculos and the Twin Dragons had almost gone to war on North Avenue. Liao, outnumbered and out of his territory, had been forced to leave under the eyes of dozens of Puerto Ricans and Mexicans who had been watching. It was a moment Liao would not forget and hadn't.

"You know who's in the hospital?" asked Kearney. "Room four floors up from where Sen was found?"

They knew.

"Del Sol," said Hanrahan.

"El Perro," Kearney confirmed, "with a bullet hole in his arm put there, so I've been told, by one of the Twin Dragons. Which means . . . ?"

"War," said Lieberman wearily.

"Want to pay a visit to your old friend, the crazy Puerto Rican?" Kearney asked Lieberman.

"As soon as . . . ," Lieberman began.

"Now would be a good time," said Kearney. "Convince him to give peace a chance. Give him the V sign with your fingers. Make nice. Scare the crap out of him. Pull him in for something creative. Stop the war before it starts."

Kearney looked at his watch.

"Go," said Kearney, putting his palms flat on the desk and looking at each of them. The three detectives got up.

"Put the chair back," Kearney said.

Hanrahan put the chair back.

Lieberman closed the door gently as they left.

"What's up his ass?" asked O'Neil, looking at the closed door.

"A lot of people who'd like to see him scoop his desk drawers into a cardboard box and head for Calumet City or points a lot further south," said Lieberman.

The squad room was just starting to get busy, but a slow busy as if perps and victims were just waking up. A few detectives were settling into their chairs, looking at computer screens, talking to people including a young black street hustler named Dewey Jackson who had witnessed a shooting the night before.

"I am leveling with you, man," Dewey said, leaning

toward a bored, large detective named Smiley whose thumbs played with his yellow suspenders as he patiently waited for Dewey to get through the preliminary denials before they got down to business.

"O'Neil," a detective named Wolniak called from a desk near the door. "You got a call on 'eight.'"

O'Neil moved to a phone on an empty desk.

"Want me to go with you to the hospital?" asked Hanrahan.

"No," said Lieberman. "Work the Morton case. I'll keep in touch. Iris okay with the baby?"

"Happy," Bill said.

"You, Father Murph?"

"Don't know, Rabbi. Who died?"

"Ida Katzman," said Lieberman.

"The one with the big gelt," said Hanrahan.

"A nice lady," said Lieberman. "Let's go get the bad guys."

"I'll give you a call," said Hanrahan.

"I don't know," said Monty Giopolus. "Maybe it's nothing. Maybe it's something. Don't want it on my conscience if it's something. You know?"

Sean O'Neil had been getting his hair cut at the Clean Cut barbershop since he was a kid and Monty's father had been doing the cutting. Then the neighborhood had been all Irish and Monty and his father had been the tolerated Greek barbers.

Now when Sean got his hair cut, there were Greeks, Jews, Italians. When the Mexicans started coming, that would be the last Monty saw of Sean O'Neil.

"What?" asked O'Neil, looking at Lieberman and Hanrahan, sure they were talking about him.

"Guy," said Monty. "Regular. Wayne Czerbiak. Must have seen him around. Kind of big. Round kid face?"

"Maybe."

"He says he's going to kill someone," said Monty.

"Who?"

"Some singer whose parents live in the neighborhood."

"Why?"

"Didn't say. Seemed kind of happy about it. Not a bad guy, but I think maybe he's not so all right in the head some reason or other."

"You believe him?"

"Don't know," said Monty. "Like I say, maybe. Look, I told you. Good citizen and everything. Cover my ass in case."

"Czerbiak have a gun?"

"How would I know?" said Monty. "Man says he has a gun is all I know."

"I'll check it out," said O'Neil.

"He's not a bad guy," said Monty.

O'Neil hung up. He had bad guys to catch. Very bad guys who had raped a cop's wife. Didn't matter she was black. She was a cop's wife. That made a difference. At least it did to him.

Lieberman stood at the foot of the hospital bed looking at the young Puerto Rican with his arm in a cast. The young man did not look happy.

"So?" asked El Perro. "What'd you think?"

"About what?"

El Perro stood at the detective's side and shook his head.

"That's my cousin Raul," said El Perro, nodding at the young man in the bed. "He's my spit and image, right?"

Raul was at least six years younger than El Perro, bore no white scar on his face, and was decidedly good-looking. El Perro could make no reasonable claim to good looks.

"The resemblance is uncanny," Lieberman said.

"Got the idea from that Saddam bastard whose ass we kicked in Iraq," said El Perro, admiring his cousin. "Doubles. Chinks can't tell us apart anyway, you know? And we can't tell them apart. So who's going to know? They come after me, see Raul, and we get them."

Lieberman nodded.

"Got another guy looks just like me," said El Perro. "For backup."

"And what if the Dragons kill Raul?" asked Lieberman.

Raul was wide-eyed and clearly frightened.

"Hey, you take chances in life, you know?" said El Perro. "We'll take care of Raul though. *Verdad,* Raul?"

Raul nodded weakly.

El Perro sat on the edge of the bed and Piedras moved to the door.

"So, you came to see how I'm doing, *Viejo.*"

"Among other things. I don't want a war with the Twin Dragons."

El Perro lifted his uncast hand and said, "Who wants war? Not me, right, Piedras?"

Lieberman looked at the big man at the door who may or may not have nodded.

"See?"

"One of the Dragons hit the sidewalk out that window yesterday," said Lieberman.

"I heard," said El Perro. "That's a coincidence, isn't it?"

"Of major proportions," said Lieberman. "I'd like to reduce the coincidences in my life. How about a meeting. You, me, Parker Liao?"

"Put Sammy Sosa in that lineup and I'll be there," El Perro said with a laugh, looking at Piedras, whose right cheek twitched in what may have been an homage to a smile. "I got nothing to say to the chink."

"Can I tell you what kind of day I'm having?" asked Lieberman, moving to the room's only chair, uncomfortable-looking aluminum and dull purple plastic.

"Sure."

"I have insomnia. I got about two hours sleep last night. I sat in the tub and read a very disappointing book. Then this morning I was severely berated by my captain for getting a prisoner I was bringing back from Yuma killed. I've got to find a man with a bad right thumbnail who doesn't want to be found. You know a man with a bad right thumbnail?"

El Perro pursed his lips and thought.

"I know a guy, Cisneros on the South Side, got no thumb, three fingers."

El Perro held up his hand with two fingers curled down to indicate which fingers Cisneros was missing.

"Wanna know how Cisneros lost his fingers, *Viejo?*"

"I'll not rest till I hear the tale."

"In a cop car," said El Perro with a smile. "You imagine that?"

"I'm trying."

"Cops were hauling him in for dealing," said El Perro, scratching his cast. "Put him in the backseat. Guy on the street got a hard-on against Cisneros. Shoots through the window of the cop car, takes out three fingers."

"I remember," said Lieberman. "Shooter have a name?"

"Everybody has a name," said El Perro. "Cisneros is your guy maybe."

Lieberman shook his head "no."

"Maybe I think of someone else. I'll have people look around."

"I'd appreciate that," said Lieberman. "Before I came here I got four calls from four different districts about men with arthritic thumbs, broken thumbs, missing thumbs, diseased thumbs, and multiple fingers."

"So that's what you're pissed off about?"

"My daughter is going to meet me for lunch."

"That's good," said El Perro.

"No, it is not," said Lieberman. "It is very bad. My daughter is not known as a carrier of good tidings, especially to me. For my daughter I am the cause of all that is ill in the world."

"She's wrong, *Viejo*," said El Perro seriously.

"I like to think so. She's having problems with her husband."

"You want him to have an accident?"

"No," said Lieberman. "It is my considered opinion that my daughter is almost certainly responsible for whatever troubles she is having. . . ."

"The black guy," said El Perro, snapping his fingers. "She's married to that black guy I saw at your house that time."

"She is."

"He seemed okay to me."

"And me," Lieberman agreed. "My grandson's bar mitzvah is coming up in a few days. It's going to cost me what I was saving to fix the roof."

"Hey, I can give you a loan," said El Perro, looking at Raul this time.

Raul tried to smile. He was no better at it than Piedras but then again Piedras wasn't facing the prospect of being gunned down on the street by the Twin Dragons.

"For reasons that I think you will understand," said Lieberman, "that is not an option."

"Oh, yeah, right," said El Perro with a too-bad shake of his head.

"We add to that the fact that I am reduced to eating the most tasteless foods in the world because of the cholesterol problem God in his infinite irony has given to me and you have a man who is definitely not in the best of humor."

"And a sit-down between me and the chinks will make you feel better?" asked El Perro, suddenly slapping Raul's leg.

Raul let out a small shriek.

"It will save some part of a day I have rued."

El Perro got up, paced the floor holding his cast against his chest with his free hand, and then, after touching Piedras's shoulder, said, "I'll sit down with them. No promises. You know? They kiss my ass and we'll make peace."

"That sounds very promising," said Lieberman. "Will you kiss his ass, too?"

"That's a joke, right? With you sometimes I can't tell. You don't smile. You don't laugh. *Viejo*, the world is a funny place."

"Hilarious," said Lieberman, standing up. "Many's the night when, unable to sleep, I've thought of something funny that happened during the day, and I laugh myself to sleep."

El Perro let out a massive sigh and said, "You know you're a crazy man? You know that? I knew it when you shot that guy in the foot in the Cuban bar. You're not crazy like me, but you're crazy."

"I'll take that as a compliment coming from one who knows," said Lieberman.

"We meet at my bingo castle," said El Perro.

"We meet someplace neutral," said Lieberman.

"No promises," El Perro said, tilting his head to one side to examine Lieberman from a slightly different perspective.

"None expected. I'll get back to you."

Lieberman stepped past Piedras and into the hall. The

next step would be to convince Parker Liao that a meeting with El Perro was worth his time. Lieberman had an idea about someone who might be able to persuade the leader of the Twin Dragons.

7

If someone were to ask Wayne why he wanted to kill Lee Cole Carter, he would have had an answer. He would have had a different answer for whoever asked the question. He had a list of answers in his head depending on the questioner and when they asked him. He wondered what, if anything, he would tell the police. He was curious about how the system would work once he was under arrest. He looked forward to being questioned, talking to a lawyer, getting a uniform, lying on a cell cot, going to trial. He would definitely plead "not guilty." No plea-bargaining. What was the point in plea-bargaining when, in some way, part of the point was seeing himself on trial?

He tried to hum "Hard Drinking Woman" as he nodded at Richie Strawn, who manned the desk, wore a uniform, and was responsible for security. Richie liked his uniform, his job. Gave him plenty of time to write poetry. He had given a lot of it to Lee Cole Carter when the famous singer came to see his parents in apartment 4G. Lee Cole had always taken the ring binder filled with what Richie was certain, or at least hoped, were lyrics for a big hit.

"Who you going to see, Wayne?" Richie asked.

"Going to shoot Lee Cole Carter."

Richie looked up at Wayne. Wayne was smiling pleasantly. Not much of a joke, but Wayne had never been known for his sense of humor. Richie shook his head saying, "Not today you're not. He just left."

"Left?"

"He'll be back tomorrow," said Richie. "Comes every day he's in town. Brings 'em stuff. Sees them an hour maybe. Looks none too happy coming in. Nice smile going out. You know how it is with parents."

Wayne didn't know how it was. He had always gotten along well with his parents.

"Tomorrow?"

"Yeah," said Richie. "Like I said. Usually in the morning. You want to come back in the morning and shoot him; I suggest around nine on the way in or ten on his way out. Don't forget to bring your camera."

"Why?"

"To shoot him."

"I've got a gun."

"Right. Right. My mistake. Come back tomorrow or leave your gun with me and I'll shoot him."

Richie shook his head.

"No," said Wayne. "I'll come back and do it myself."

Hanrahan and O'Neil found Hugh Morton at his duplex home two blocks from Lake Michigan in the Lincoln Park area. The building was squeezed tight between two apartment buildings. The yellow bricks of the 1950s two-family building had recently been sandblasted. The small patch of grass was surrounded by a knee-high black painted wrought-iron fence in front of a small well-trimmed front lawn.

Hanrahan had pushed the bell. A woman had answered. She was the color of light coffee, about forty, hair pulled tightly back. She was a beauty dressed in a black business suit touched off by pearl earrings and a pearl necklace.

"Is Detective Morton home?" asked Hanrahan.

She pursed her full lips, looked at the two men and clearly pegged them for cops.

"I think he'd like to be alone with his son right now. He's heading over to the hospital to be with his wife in a few minutes," she said, not standing back for them to enter.

"And you are . . . ?" asked O'Neil.

"Denise's sister," she said.

"Detective Morton's wife is Denise?" asked Hanrahan.

She didn't answer, though both detectives sensed that she could have come back with something sharp and very sarcastic.

"She is," the woman said. "Are you handling the case?"

"We are," said Bill. "We'd like a word with Detective Morton. Please. Just ask him if he'll see us. If he says 'no,' we'll go away."

She considered the request, looked down and then said, "Wait here."

When she was gone, the door closed, O'Neil said, "We'll go away?"

"Yeah," said Hanrahan.

"We've got a fucking murder investigation going on here," said O'Neil. "Kearney's scratching at our backs with dirty nails and you say 'we'll go away.'"

"And we will," said Bill.

"To the hospital to talk to the victim, right?"

"We'll see," said Hanrahan.

The door opened again. Hugh Morton stood there, tall, blue slacks, blue shirt, and blood-red tie.

"Hanrahan, right?" he said evenly.

"Right. This is Sean O'Neil."

No handshakes. A nod from Morton.

"It's our case," said Hanrahan.

"It's my wife," Morton replied. "My child."

"I know . . . ," Hanrahan said.

"Not really," said Morton. "You don't really know. Take out your pad. I'll give you what I have."

Hanrahan pulled out his pad. A man with a briefcase walked by on the sidewalk and looked up at the three men.

Morton's eyes followed the man.

"Three of them," he said. "All white. In their twenties. One had a shaved head, goatee, wore a black T-shirt, something shiny, jeans, washed out, belt with a buckle shaped like a bird's head. The second was skinny, white shirt with a guy carrying a guitar on it, image faded. Second guy had an earring, right ear, plain. Third guy was short, walked with a swagger, mouth open, looked retarded. Shirt orange with a blue sword on it. None of them used names. She didn't see their car. They came up from behind her and pushed her between two cars."

Hanrahan quickly took notes.

"Now," said Morton, "that's what she saw. I didn't ask her how she felt, how many times, or . . . If you have any other questions for her, tell them to me and I'll ask her."

"We'll have to—," O'Neil began but Hanrahan put out a hand to stop him.

"Okay," Bill said to Morton.

"Anything else?" asked Morton.

"Anything we can do?" asked Hanrahan.

"Yes," said Morton. "Find them before I do because if I find them first, it's going to be messy."

"Won't help to do that," said Bill.

"Yes, it will," said Morton. "It'll help a lot and you know it. I've got to go now."

Morton closed the door.

"If we move real slow on this," O'Neil said as they moved back toward their car, "Morton will close it out for us and save Cook County the cost of a trial and the State of Illinois the expense of keeping the bastards locked up for the rest of their lives."

"One problem with that," said Bill, opening the car door on the driver's side.

"Yeah?"

"That ends it for Morton," Bill said. "He'll go down and out."

"His choice," said O'Neil, getting into the car.

"Not if we find the bastards first," said Hanrahan.

Lieberman sat across from his daughter Lisa in the back booth of the T&L deli, the one near the restrooms, the one he sat in facing the door to the street whenever he could get it. If he called ahead, his brother Maish reserved it for him. He had called ahead.

Lisa sat silently, coffee cup in both hands, looking at the warm brown liquid. She was pretty, a little too thin, her straight black hair long and brushed to catch the light. She wasn't quite as pretty as her mother. Lisa had just a hint of the Lieberman stock that gave her face a slight sadness even when she was happy, though Lieberman could remember few times when his daughter was truly happy.

There were five customers in the T&L and only four *alter cockers* at the table near the window. The *alter cockers* were debating the future of mankind, having just disposed of the heady issue of whether Hank Greenberg or Sandy Koufax was the greatest Jewish baseball player who ever lived. The vote had been split with Howie Chen wavering till the last second and voting for Koufax, to which Herschel Rosen, a Greenberg worshiper, had said, "Traitor. You shouldn't get a vote. Name even one, even one Chinese baseball player."

"Cy Yung," said Howie with a straight face.

Louis Roth sputtered with laughter, his thick glasses flying from his nose. Morris Hurwitz reached out and grabbed them before they hit the table.

"Lieberman," Rosen called. "You make the call. The greatest Jewish baseball player."

"Rod Carew," said Lieberman.

"He was a convert," Rosen said with mock disgust. "He was a *shvartze*."

"A Jew is a Jew," said Hurwitz, the psychologist.

"Genetics comes into this equation," said Rosen.

"I thought we were talking religion?" said Roth.

"I thought we were talking baseball," countered Rosen.

"You are hopeless, all hopeless," said Roth. "If I didn't like the Nova lox here, I'd let you all try to make it through life on your own. You going to Ida Katzman's funeral?"

"I'm going," said Lieberman.

"Where's Irish?" asked Rosen. "I thought you were joined at the hip. Who was the surgeon who performed the miracle of separation? I want to see him with my wife."

"The surgeon was a woman," said Abe.

"Then I'm not taking any chances," said Rosen.

And then the *alter cockers* turned their attention to saving the world.

"Suicide bombers," Roth declared.

"Again with suicide bombers?" asked Rosen.

"I thought we agreed to call them homicide bombers," said Howie.

"Semantics is not the issue," said Hurwitz. "We need solutions, not more questions."

"Who asked a question?" said Roth, pointing to his chest.

"I'm in favor of building the wall," said Rosen.

"Second the motion," said Roth, agreeing with Rosen one of the few times in his life. "Lieberman the cop, what do you think?"

"Make the Palestinians rich and they'll stop bombing."

"And how do you propose making them rich?" asked Roth.

"Make the Saudis give them billions, build factories, start industries," said Lieberman.

"They don't want money," said Howie Chen. "They want Israel to go away."

Lieberman shrugged and slowly drank his coffee and forced himself to take small bites of his omelet filled with mushrooms and done on the soft side the way he tolerated them. The *alter cockers* kept up the discussion.

"So?" Lieberman asked his daughter, sneaking a peek at his watch.

"So?" Lisa answered, looking up at him.

"Your husband's not coming to the bar mitzvah?"

"No," she said. "I . . . I can't look at him."

Lieberman said nothing, took a very small forkful of omelet and judged that he had half an omelet left to eat. A slice of cantaloupe sat untouched on his plate.

"You want to know why?" she said, her eyes meeting his in a challenge he was sure would lay guilt on the table.

"Why?" he asked.

"Guilt," she said.

"What's he guilty of?" asked Lieberman.

"Nothing. I'm guilty," she said. "He forgave me for that, that business with the intern last year."

Lieberman caught himself before he could make a comment on the word *business*. It would not do to open that door.

"I see it in his eyes," she said. "His forgiving eyes, his gentle brown eyes, his knowing smile. I can't live being forgiven, constantly forgiven."

Lieberman nodded and said, "You want him to hit you? Yell?"

"Yes," she said. "But it's not in him. I need closure. He won't give it to me. He can't give it to me."

"It's *nuc-lear*," said Hurwitz at the *alter cocker* table. "Not *nucular*."

"Jimmy Carter was wrong?" said Roth.

"Bush was wrong?" added Rosen.

"Wrong is wrong," Hurwitz insisted. "You want to save the world, you start by pronouncing words correctly, particularly important words. That's all I'm saying."

Maish waddled up to Abe and Lisa's table and freshened their coffee. He touched his niece's cheek and she touched her uncle's stubby hand.

"You going to the funeral, Maish?" asked Lieberman.

"I'll be there."

"No trouble?" asked Abe.

Maish shrugged and held up the coffeepot. Since Maish's son David had been murdered a few years earlier, he had taken to battle with God and Rabbi Wass whenever the opportunity presented itself. It wasn't that he had become an atheist. An atheist has no one to do battle with over the injustice of life. Maish believed in God. He just didn't like Him very much anymore.

"No trouble," agreed Maish, but Abe wasn't sure.

He watched his brother carry the pot over to the *alter cocker* table where Rosen asked him, "Who was more important, Einstein or FDR?"

Abe didn't hear the answer. Lisa was speaking. He missed the first part of what she was saying but caught ". . . I can't live with it."

"You can't?"

"Unless he changes," she said softly.

"Changes?"

"Talk to him," Lisa said, looking away. "He'll listen to you. He likes you. He respects you."

All three of which, Abe was sure, Lisa did not feel about her relationship with her father.

"I'll talk to him," Abe said. "I'll advise marriage counseling."

"It won't work," she said.

"Then doormats anonymous," said Abe.

"You always think being funny will get you out of responsibility," she said with a disgust with which Abe was quite familiar.

"I never think being funny will get me out of responsibility," he said. "My hope is that seeing the possibility will keep me from depression."

"Will you do it?" she asked, an ultimatum more than a request. "You owe that to me."

Lieberman wasn't sure why he owed it to his daughter, but he said, "Yes."

"When?"

"Tonight," he said. "I'll call him."

"He's home at seven Pacific time," she said. "He never stops for a drink, picks up women, sneaks off to a movie. Seven."

"I'll call him," Lieberman said, finishing his omelet. "You're going to be here for Barry's bar mitzvah?"

"Abe," she said, leaning forward. "Barry is my son. Of course I'll be here."

Abe said nothing, nothing about the times she had not been there for her children, nothing about the fact that she had turned them over to Abe and Bess to raise. There was nothing to say that would make the situation better.

"And the speech?" Abe asked.

"I don't like it," she said. "But I'll be quiet. He's already learned it."

"What would you like him to say?"

"I don't know," Lisa said with a sigh. "The world is . . . I don't know."

"You done?" he asked. "I mean with your coffee?"

Lisa nodded, wiped her mouth with her napkin and stood up.

On Devon in front of the T&L, Abe fished his car keys out of his pants pocket. The door of the deli opened behind him and he turned.

Howie Chen, short, heavy, large dark sacs under his eyes that had been there as long as Lieberman had known him, said, "A word?"

"Sure."

Howie looked at Lisa, who said, "I'll meet you at the car."

When she was just out of earshot, Howie said, "I heard about the death of David Sen. I know his grandfather, Chang, a good man."

Abe watched a black-coated and dark-bearded Orthodox Jew in a black hat walk by avoiding meeting their eyes.

"Victor tells me you're working on it," Howie went on.

"There's trouble," said Abe. "I'm doing what I can to see there's as little as possible."

Howie shook his head in understanding.

"Twin Dragons," said Howie. "My nephew Raymond is one of them, my sister Anna's youngest boy. She says they're talking about war with the Puerto Ricans. Raymond has a . . . what should I call it, a loyalty, almost like a religion. The Twin Dragons mean everything to him. I don't want him to be a martyr in a stupid war."

"I'll do what I can," said Lieberman.

"Honor is not overrated," said Howie, "but it is often misplaced."

"You get that in a fortune cookie?"

Howie smiled. Abe did the same. Abe's smile was much smaller.

"May I make a suggestion?" asked Howie.

"Make it."

"You might want to seek Mr. Woo's advice."

"I may," Abe agreed, and the two men departed, Abe for a tense drive to pick up Bess for the funeral, Howie to return to his seat at the *alter cocker* table where the old men were heatedly solving the problems of the world, which, Howie Chen thought, was much easier than stopping a gang war.

Cowboy Faubus stood up at the bar of Vernon's Tap in Yuma. The music was country, loud, Waylon Jennings. There was also a baseball game on the television over the bar. The sound was off. The Diamondbacks were ahead of the Red Sox 3–1 in the sixth. Waylon Jennings and the score of the game were all right with the Cowboy, whose hat lay on the bar.

He brushed back his long hair, emptied his beer glass, and said, "It's the fingers."

He demonstrated what he meant, holding the glass in front of the man on the stool next to him. There were two reasons to hold it close: the dim light of the bar, and the fact that the man was about three drinks ahead of the Cowboy.

"Split finger like so. Knuckler like so. Trick is to hide it from the batter."

The man on the stool nodded "yes" as if he understood what the hell the Cowboy was talking about.

"And the fastball and slider," said Faubus. "Subtle difference, you know? See?"

"Uh-huh," said the man on the stool.

The Cowboy sighed in frustration.

"If I had a ball, I could show you exactly."

He could show the man, show the world, how to hold a baseball for every pitch, including the screwball. He used to have a great screwball, spinning the ball out instead of in. Great pitch. Short career. Tears the hell out of your shoulder.

The telephone behind the bar rang.

"Martinez is the best damn pitcher ever," the drunk on the stool said. "Ever."

The phone rang again. Larry the bartender picked it up.

"You know what you know?" asked Faubus. "You know? You don't know shit? Martinez is damn good but—"

"Cowboy," said Larry. "For you."

He handed the phone over to Faubus.

"Yeah."

"How did it go?" asked the caller.

"Like we planned," Faubus said. "Perfect. Went down just as planned. You should have seen me. Wish you could have. Threw the cop curves he didn't even see coming."

"Thanks," said the caller.

"You'd do it for me," said the Cowboy.

"I would."

"You take care of yourself," said Faubus, and the caller hung up. So did Cowboy, who turned back to the drunk. "Where was I?"

"Screwball," said the drunk.

"She's a cop's wife."

Easy Dan spoke with a large chocolate-chip cookie in one hand and his eyes on the television set in Blue's living room.

"Look," Easy Dan said, pointing his cookie toward the screen.

Blue Berg had been sitting in his grandmother's chair, the one with faded pink flowers on silky green material. His right leg had been draped over one of the arms and he had been staring at the wall, biting a knuckle and feeling trapped.

He looked, but he didn't care. He didn't listen to the talking head of a blond woman with too-red lips and amazing white teeth being serious about what Blue, Easy Dan, and Comedy had done to the woman the night before.

Comedy had called the woman a nigger. Blue had slapped him so hard that Comedy had gone to his knees spitting blood.

"I told you none of that racist crap," Blue had said in the alley after they had raped the woman and were heading toward the street, the crying kid behind them kneeling on both knees next to his mother.

"Sorry," Comedy said, getting up.

"He's sorry," Easy Dan had said. "Let's just get the hell out of here."

"Everybody's the same," Blue had said. "No spics, no chinks, no dagos, no nothing. People are goddamn people.

Women are all the same. They get no passes for being white or red or fucking fudge ripple."

When they got in the car, Blue had sat behind the wheel, fingers gripping tightly, not saying what he felt and thought, that if his own whore of a mother who had run out on him when he was five ever showed up again, he'd do to her what he did to them all, young, old, anything.

He knew it was an obsession, an addiction he had come across, welcomed, been surprised. Came from nowhere. Burst out. A girl. Young. Easy Dan and Comedy were with him. They were heading for who knows where. Cruising, listening to the beat-beat-beat of a heavy metal band.

He didn't tell them what he was going to do. He had just grabbed her, pulled her into the car, his head pounding with anger, his palm over her mouth.

That was the first. What? A month ago? Two months? It wouldn't last forever or maybe it would. They would catch him, the cops, or maybe they wouldn't. Maybe he should throw some things in the car, drive anywhere with or without Dan and Comedy, start it all again. But he knew he wouldn't do it.

Screw it.

Comedy came out of the kitchen with a bottle of Dr Pepper in his hand, a grin on his face, his usual swagger-bounce. Blue heard the front door of the house open. He couldn't see who it was. Probably his father or his grandmother wondering where he was when they needed him. Blue had ignored the ringing phone.

Whoever it was stepped around the corner of the little entry hall and stood facing the Blue Glee Club.

Wayne went home. He wasn't disappointed. It was a nice day and the weatherman on WGN, Tom Skilling, had said it would be just as nice tomorrow.

Wayne tucked the gun into a drawer and went to his worktable. It was big, flat, smooth white wood with paint stains from years of work. He put a Lee Cole Carter CD in the player his cousin Anton had given him last Christmas.

The sign Wayne worked on was for the St. Stephen's rummage sale. Each year he made a bigger sign, more colorful, always with a cross, always with a basket of clothes, toys, and books flowing out of it. Date, time, and place in the corner in bright red. He had charged them nothing for the sign but took a gift certificate for five dollars in rummage-sale goods.

When Wayne's father had been alive, the two of them had planned the signs, discussed them, came up with new ideas that would attract buyers. They had tried religious appeal. It hadn't worked. They had tried the hope of salvation for good deeds. That hadn't worked. They had tried a simple bright shout of *bargain* and that had been reasonably successful. Between the two of them, they had made eight signs to put around the neighborhood, including the window of the Clean Cut barbershop. Now Wayne made only five signs, but that seemed to be enough.

"Whiskey don't dull the pain," he sang along with the man he planned to kill the next day.

Wayne laid down a splash of blue and stood back to admire it, singing "but it sure does make a stain that covers my poor heart like a layer of tin."

He sighed, satisfied. When he finished the sign, he would make another, one for himself. The walls of the small house were covered with posterlike signs, signs and posters his father would never have allowed, not that his father was a hard man, not that he would forbid, but his disapproval would be there and he would just take them down without a word to his son if it had to come to that.

There were six posters on the wall of the bright, sunny room with four tall, uncovered windows.

One poster was of a man with a guitar standing on the moon at night, cowboy hat on his tilted-back head. Wayne was good at drawing people. This one looked a little like Willie Nelson. The yellow words against the night sky were *It's all got to end.*

That was the earliest of the posters. Wayne had advanced from such pessimism as his mission slowly emerged.

Poster two was of a couple dancing on top of a car at the Lake Michigan shore down by Fiftieth Street. It was night again. The couple was wearing formal clothes like the ones they wore to the Sullivan High School prom, which Wayne had not attended though he had done the posters. The words, in blue outlined in white, were *Never Stop Dancing.*

Poster three was a trio of grinning dwarfs dressed in zoot suits and lined up with guns in their hands facing whoever might be looking at them. The words, black against a white strip, were, *We represent the Lollipop Kids*.

Poster four, three weeks old: The face of a man with his mouth opened wide, wider than humanly possible and inside the mouth were marbles, all different colors, all different sizes, hundreds of them and over the man's head, white on purple, were the words, *There's always room for one more*.

Poster five, last week: All red with a single burst of white in the center that sprayed droplets in all directions. One word in black: *Soon*.

Poster six, two days ago: All black, no words.

"Can't melt it with a blowtorch," he sang softly. "Can't chip away with the hammer of loss. Can't melt that hard, thick layer with words that sound like love."

And then Lee Cole Carter sang, "Believe it."

And Wayne Czerbiak sang back with the backup group, "I believe it."

Lee Cole Carter sang louder, "Believe it."

Wayne Czerbiak sang back louder, "I believe it."

And one last time, Lee Cole Carter sang, "You better believe it."

And Wayne had belted out, "I better believe it" unaware that he was spraying red paint on the windows and walls from the brush in his right hand.

The chapel was crowded at Rosenzwieg's Funeral Parlor. Ida Katzman was laid out in a simple wooden coffin, on a blue-and-white–cloth-covered table. The coffin, as she had dictated to Kenneth Rosenzweig many years earlier, was closed.

Rabbi Wass stood behind a wooden podium, tallis over his shoulder, and black yarmulke on his head. The tallis kept slipping and Rabbi Wass kept adjusting both it and his glasses. He had no notes before him as he watched the last few people enter the chapel.

He waited while Morrie Greenblatt, long retired from the furniture business and almost eighty, showed people to open seats and gently urged them to settle down. Morrie was still taller than most of the people he ushered, but time had worn the space between his bones and he no longer towered.

The last to arrive were Maish and Yetta Lieberman. Rabbi Wass tried not to meet Maish's eyes. He silently prayed that the bitter deli owner would not use this occasion to launch a challenge to him and to God.

The rabbi let his eyes wander toward Abe and Bess Lieberman and their daughter. They caught the message and made room for Maish and Yetta at their side where, God willing, they would rein in the heresy.

After a prayer in Hebrew and an amen from the more than one hundred people gathered, Rabbi Wass said, "Ida Rebecca Katzman, beloved wife of Hyman Katzman, *alevai shalom*, dear friend of those of us gathered here, giver of her wise counsel to our congregation, the firm and devout foundation of the growth and well-being of Temple Mir Shavot, will be missed. She lived a full life, an often difficult life, but also an often rewarding life. She lived with dignity and went on in peace. She asked me specifically that when she died the service be short, the speeches minimal, and the burial quick. She asked for only one person to make a statement if he wished. Abraham Lieberman, do you wish to speak?"

Abe rose, adjusted the black yarmulke, and moved past his wife and daughter to the aisle. The call was not unexpected. Rabbi Wass had warned him in advance when he greeted him at the entrance to the chapel. Nothing had come to mind to say about Ida Katzman. He walked slowly to the small platform, touched the coffin on the way, and stood behind the podium as Rabbi Wass moved aside.

The room was silent. Lieberman's eyes scanned the familiar faces.

"Ida Katzman had a lot of money," he said. "Most people couldn't see beyond that to the woman with eyes that were always at peace. I never saw her angry, never heard her say a negative thing about anyone even when they sorely cried for it. She looked as if she carried a secret. She talked as if she understood what you were really thinking, not what you said. I'll miss her. I'll miss the tapping of her cane when she entered a room. I'll miss her calm voice."

Lieberman paused, looked down at his hands gripping the edges of the podium, noticed the brown spots of age and sun and said, "That's the eulogy part. What I'll remember about Ida is the off-color joke she told me once over coffee and a *hamantaschen* at Purim. She laughed. Never heard her laugh like that before. She laughed and slapped my back and I laughed with her, not because the joke was so damn funny, but because I saw an Ida Katzman I didn't know, an Ida Katzman who felt comfortable enough with me to let herself show through. A small confidence, sure, but a confidence. I want to remember that laugh and feel that slap on the back when I think of her. That's it."

Lieberman left the platform, touched the coffin again, and went back to his place beside Bess, who whispered, "Except for the 'damn,' you were all right, Lieberman."

Ida Katzman had no living relatives. Her sister, brother, and parents had died in the Holocaust. She and Hyman had not been able to have children. So, Bess, as president of the congregation, and Rabbi Wass, as spiritual leader, shook hands with the mourners as they departed.

Off to the side with Lisa, Lieberman nodded as people

congratulated him on his eulogy. Irving Hammel, attorney, the youngest member of the congregation's board, the man who would be president, shook Abe's hand and said, "Can you and Bess be in Rabbi Wass's study tomorrow morning at nine?"

"I've got—," Lieberman began.

"It's important, Abe."

"We'll be there."

And Hammel was gone with the crowd.

There were sixteen cars behind the hearse that went to the cemetery in Northfield. They drove down a narrow stone drive, past tastefully placed simple tablets set in softly rolling hills. The trees were small, green; a slight breeze was blowing.

They passed the section called Mamre where Abe's father and mother were buried and drove to a newer section where a few people had already gathered next to a neatly dug hole. A dozen plastic folding chairs were set a few feet beyond the hole and older women were being led to them.

Slowly the pallbearers, including Abe, removed the casket from the hearse. It was light. There had not been much left of Ida Katzman but her spirit and she had insisted that the box in which she was buried be of simple pine.

They placed the casket on a platform near the grave and stepped back.

Prayers, some soft weeping, handfuls of dirt dropped on the casket after it was lowered, and everyone stepped back.

Across the small chasm of the grave, behind the old women in the folding chairs, amid the mourners standing solemnly, Lieberman sensed someone looking at him. He looked up and met the eyes of a tall heavyset man in a dark suit. The man had thick black hair and wore rimless spectacles.

The man held up his right hand and half turned it so that

Lieberman could see the distinctive brown and gnarled thumbnail.

Rabbi Wass softly said his final prayer and everyone, including the man with the gnarled thumb, said, "Amen."

Berg was behind the counter when Hanrahan and O'Neil went in. He didn't look happy to see them.

"You have a son," said O'Neil.

It wasn't a question.

An old couple was sitting on stools by the window looking out at traffic. The old man, cheek full of cheeseburger, Pepsi in hand in a plastic cup with a straw, glanced at the three men over his shoulder.

"I have a son," Bert Berg, said wiping his hands on his apron.

"He works here," Hanrahan said.

"Sometimes."

"His name is Paul," said Hanrahan.

Berg nodded.

"He has a record," said O'Neil.

Berg didn't argue.

"Where is he now?" asked Hanrahan.

"I don't know," said the man. "Home maybe. He's due here to relieve me at three."

"The woman who was here yesterday?" asked O'Neil.

"My mother. Pauly's grandmother."

"You know why we're here, don't you, Mr. Berg?"

"Not the woman last night," he pleaded.

"I think we'd better talk to your son," said O'Neil.

"It's not real," said Berg, looking at the policeman. "He works hard, never forgets my mother's birthday or Mother's Day."

He looked at the two policemen, dropped his shoulders and added, "But that doesn't mean anything, does it?"

The policemen didn't answer.

"You're not listed in the telephone directory," said Hanrahan. "No record of a house in your name. We need your address."

"House is my mother's."

He gave them the address.

"To do that to someone," Berg said. "He's . . . Where does it come from?"

The policemen had no answer.

"Don't call your house, Mr. Berg," O'Neil said.

"I'll close up. Come with you."

He started to take off his apron.

"Better if you just stayed here for now," said Hanrahan.

"Right," Berg said, dazed.

The policemen left quickly.

"Too damned easy," said O'Neil. "If we can find him this easy, Morton might be ahead of us."

"Might," agreed Hanrahan.

They got in their car. Hanrahan opened the window and put the flashing light on the roof. They had six blocks to go. It took them three minutes.

The small redbrick two-story bungalow was on a side street with shaded trees and only a few parked cars. They pulled up in front of the house, turned off the light, and stepped out, guns in hand. Across the street a young mother was pushing a stroller. She saw the two men and turned quickly around.

A blue car was parked at the curb. A small stuffed monkey dangled from the rearview mirror.

Three stone steps up. The door wasn't locked. O'Neil

pushed it open. Hanrahan, weapon leveled, stepped in and shouted "Police."

He took a step to his right into the living room, O'Neil just behind him.

In front of them stood an old woman, her hair disheveled, her mouth open, her arms held wide, palms bathed in blood. Her blue dress was splotched with dark patches of blood.

Behind her were two figures, one in a chair, leg draped over an arm, eyes dead and staring, face covered with blood. On the floor a few feet away, facedown, lay another figure in an unbuttoned flannel shirt, a Rorschach of blood on his back.

"He ran," the woman cried, pointing to a door across the room behind a table in a dining area.

"Back," said Hanrahan running across the room, knowing O'Neil was going back through the front door.

Hanrahan bumped into a chair, knocked over another, pushed open a door and found himself in a small kitchen. The back door was wide open. Hanrahan jumped out, knees feeling the pain. O'Neil was coming around the side of the building and pointing his gun at a fence.

"I think I saw him go over," he shouted. "Saw something."

The two policemen ran for the fence. O'Neil went over first. Hanrahan's knees slowed him down but he made it over. They stood side by side looking around. They were in another yard, green with a single tree. From the tree a swing swayed gently.

O'Neil dashed toward the front of the house before them. Hanrahan went back over the fence and hobbled toward the open back door.

He found the old woman standing not where he had left her but facing the bloody corpse in the chair. Her hands were on her face.

"Mrs. Berg," he said, putting his gun back in his holster.

He put his arm around her and guided her into the small hallway and out the front door. She whimpered and took quick shallow breaths. When she moved her hands from her face, her cheeks were crimson with bloody prints.

"My Pauly," she said, looking at him.

Hanrahan looked at the bodies. Neither had a goatee or shaven head.

"Your grandson did this?" asked Hanrahan.

O'Neil appeared from the side of the house shaking his head to let Hanrahan know that he hadn't caught up with whoever had gone out the back door.

"Mrs. Berg," Hanrahan repeated. "Did your grandson do this?"

"Was it a black man?" asked O'Neil.

"Sean," Hanrahan warned.

"Was he . . . ?" she asked, looking at O'Neil. "Yes, I think. I don't know."

"But you'd know him again if you saw him?" O'Neil prompted.

"Know him?" she said looking at the two men without recognition.

"Call it in," Hanrahan said. "We'll get her to the hospital."

A few people were watching now from across the street including the young woman with the stroller. Mrs. Berg looked at them puzzled.

"Pauly was supposed to work this afternoon," she said as Hanrahan guided her to the car.

"I know," said the detective.

"Someone should tell my Bert," she said.

"We'll take care of it."

She stopped and looked up at him, her cheeks scarlet, finger-painted.

"Do you know what Pauly did last night?"

Hanrahan knew.

"You know where your grandson is, Mrs. Berg?" Hanrahan asked.

She looked toward the kitchen door and closed her eyes.

At three minutes after three in a hospital bed in Yuma, Billy Johnstone sat talking to the man who had shot him. Detective Martin Parsons asked him lots of questions. Billy answered most of them, but not the ones that counted.

"What happened to that little Jew detective?" he asked.

"Went back to Chicago," said Parsons.

Johnstone held up his right hand and showed Parsons his thumb.

"Looking for the man," Johnstone said.

"Yeah."

"You aren't much of a shot," Johnstone said. "How much you practice?"

"Couple of times a month."

"I was counting on you killing me," Johnstone said.

"Sorry," said Parsons.

"Hell, I killed that Gower straight off and I've never fired a gun before in my life," said Johnstone. "And I hit him square and dead. And my hand was shaky and my eyesight isn't all that good anymore."

"Next time I'll be sure to kill you," Parsons said flatly.

Johnstone cocked his head and looked at the young detective and asked, "You're joking with me, right?"

"Wouldn't count on that," said Parsons with a smile. "You're joking with me, right?"

"Count on it," said Johnstone.

Parsons was silent.

"*Price Is Right* is on," Johnstone said, looking up at the television. The sound was off. "Game channel."

"Let's talk," Parsons repeated.

"We've been talking."

"Let's talk some more," said Parsons.

Johnstone clicked off the television and muttered, "Hell, they're all long dead anyhow. Watching dead people play games," he said. "All right, let's talk."

At three minutes after four, which was three minutes after three in Yuma, Mr. Woo sat in the rear showroom of Alexander Pietros's gallery on Michigan Avenue. The showroom's steel door, tastefully painted to look as if it were wood, was locked and bolted. Pietros had just ordered his nephew Marcos to bring out a stone carving. The carving, a rough, eyeless human head with a long face, was on a cart, resting on purple velvet, a touch Mr. Woo found condescending.

Marcos pushed the cart noiselessly in front of the old man, who nodded. Alexander Pietros nodded, too, and made a twisting motion with his right hand. Marcos responded by slowly turning the cart so Mr. Woo could examine the carving from all sides.

No one said what it was or where it had come from. No one had to. Mr. Woo knew that it was Mesopotamian and had been stolen during the war in Iraq from a museum in Baghdad. Its value was in its age and history and not its beauty. To possess it was to have in one's power a relic that proved human history was vulnerable to the furtive fingers of a thief. To possess it was to say that one had it in his power to preserve or erase a small piece of the past.

Fingers could reach out to protect it, worship it, want to preserve it to prove their own ties to a history they considered ancient and part of a lineage far longer than the Book of Numbers. Or hands could lift it high and dash it against a floor shattering it into bits, pieces, shards that meant nothing.

Woo wanted the rather homely piece not to destroy it, but to know that he could destroy it if he wished. He would dream of curators and archeologists reaching out to him as he stood on a platform with the worn carving on a fragile pedestal from which he could push it to crushed powder on a marble floor.

That dream was worth much to Woo, who had been born a thief and a beggar in Shanghai. He was prepared to pay whatever was required to own it.

El Perro fingered his scar with one hand and looked down at a white Ping-Pong ball with the letter *B* and the number *2* on it. The Ping-Pong ball rested on a turned-over Dr Pepper bottle cap.

El Perro adjusted his cast and sling and dropped *B2* into the wire basket in front of him. He was well enough to call numbers tonight. He would have the cast cut off before doing so even though he had been told that it had to stay on for at least another two weeks. Everyone knew the Twin Dragons had shot El Perro. He wanted to show them that a Chinese bullet meant nothing to him.

Dr. Luis Algado would come in an hour. That would give El Perro time to flex his fingers and will himself to ignore the pain he anticipated but didn't fear.

From the stage in the large hall on North Avenue he looked down past the tables as Martin Lozada Cruz came in, closing the doors behind him, and hurried forward.

"Two of them at a place in Little Vietnam," said Cruz.

"Which ones?" asked El Perro.

"I don't know their names," said Cruz. "But they are Twin Dragons. They are with girls. You want them dead?"

"Before bingo."

Cruz nodded and turned to leave.

"Martin," El Perro called. "You know it is a good thing to be alive."

"*Sí*," said Martin, turning.

"But being alive don't mean shit if you don't take chances," said El Perro. "You don't take chances, how do you know you're alive."

"*Sí*," said Martin Cruz with a smile, though he wasn't sure if he understood what El Perro had said.

As he left the hall, Cruz heard the turning of the basket of numbered Ping-Pong balls behind him.

At three minutes after four, Parker Liao sat in the backseat of a black Mazda. The windows of the Mazda were tinted and dark. The car was parked on Argyle Street across from a Vietnamese restaurant called Saigon Flower.

Besides the driver, two other young Chinese, all wearing dark silk suits with compatible but not matching ties, sat waiting.

"You are certain?" asked Liao.

"Certain," the driver said. "The Puerto Rican worms saw Chao, Winn, and the two girls enter."

Liao said nothing.

He was sure they would come. The Puerto Ricans were stupid, brave but stupid. They had been led into a trap thinking they were the ones who were trapping. The double turn appealed to Liao. In the next hour, the crazy Puerto Rican would know he had been beaten in this battle.

Liao would rub El Perro's scarred face in the defeat.

He had no illusions about El Perro giving up. He did not want him to give up. He wanted him humiliated and on his knees in front of him.

The Puerto Rican wouldn't beg for his life. He had pride. It was not quite honor, but it was an animal pride that Liao could appreciate.

He would let El Perro utter defiance and curses. And then he would cut his throat and have his body dumped on a street in his neighborhood.

And that would be soon.

And that would be a very good day.

At three minutes after four, Blue Berg was strung out and in need of something, anything. Comedy was dead. Easy Dan was dead. Blue was alive, shaking and sitting on a toilet in McDonald's.

The stall door was locked. He could hear people come and go. The sound of peeing in a urinal and the flush and rush. The sound of flushing in the next stall.

Blue's pants were up, belted. He tried to think. Blue just didn't believe life was going anywhere but right here and now. Life was a series of flats and blasts and Blue knew how to find the blast that would last, at least a little while.

Blue looked at his hands. He had kept them in his pockets as much as possible before he washed them in the fountain in the park. He never drank from the fountain. The water came out too low and to get a drink you had to put your lips on the rusting metal spout. Who knew whose mouth had last touched that spout. But he had washed his hands trying to get the blood out.

Someone washing his hands in the restroom coughed. Blue shivered.

A lot of the blood had come out when he had washed. Not all but a lot. Now Blue's hands were just pink.

He hadn't looked back when he left his house through the back door. He had heard someone call "police" but he hadn't looked back. He had run through the back door, gone over the back fence, run around a redbrick house with a swing in the back, run across a street, hidden behind some trash cans for a few minutes, and then run to the park.

He didn't want to think about what was in his pocket, but he really had no choice. He could have thrown it away, wiped his fingerprints off and thrown the gun away. He should have, but he couldn't. It sat heavy in his pocket, covered by his extra-large blue T-shirt, which had a few spots on it that might be anything, but were certainly blood.

Staying in the toilet forever was not an option though it wouldn't hurt to stay here for a few hours more. In those few hours, he could try to think of what to do. *Try* was the operative word. He had no illusions about succeeding.

He counted the money in his worn wallet and front pocket: twenty-four dollars and sixty-three cents. Can't get far on twenty-four dollars and sixty-three cents. Besides, he couldn't think of anyplace to go except his aunt Henny's apartment in Palatine. They wouldn't let him in. He knew that. He could break in through the bathroom window. He had done it many times before, but then what? And how would he get there? His car was still parked in front of the house. Maybe he could steal a car and—

Knock at the stall door.

"Someone in there?"

It was a man. He sounded black. Deep voice. Voice of a preacher, a cop, Mr. Dwight the principal at Lake View High where Blue had gone to school, more or less, for two years. The principal is a pal. That's how you spell it, *pal* not *ple*. Why did he remember that? He didn't remember fuckin' much else.

The stall door rattled.

"Someone in there?" the man asked again, knocking at the door.

"Yeah," Blue managed.

"Been in there a long time," came the voice. "You okay?"

"Yeah."

Were there any bullets left in the gun? He could take it out, pull the trigger hoping the bullets would go through the stall door. Then he could run. He just sat feeling cold.

"Well, quit playing with yourself or whatever you're doing and make it snappy."

"Yeah."

The man's footsteps clapped away on the tile floor. Blue could hear the washroom door opened and closed. Blue tried to stand. His legs were weak. He tried again holding on to the side of the stall. This time he made it. He reached for the bolt and realized that he hadn't the slightest idea of what he was going to do when it swung open.

At three minutes after four, the mayor of Chicago sat behind his desk drinking a cup of coffee, listening to the traffic outside and the three people across from him who had carefully rehearsed their presentation.

They were all black. One, Estelle Rives, was a former alderwoman and the leader of the group that had come with a carefully couched demand that something be done about TerrorTown, the area of the South Side where drug gangs ruled the streets, people hid at night, and police, when they had to go there, were less than welcome and sometimes shot.

"And you have a plan?" the mayor said.

"We have a plan," Estelle Rives said, looking at the lean elderly man at her side with a professorial air, thick glasses, and white hair.

The man, Dr. Frank Roland, handed the mayor a neatly stapled, thin sheaf of paper with a red cover. The mayor took it, put down his coffee, and opened the stapled plan.

"Bottom line?" the mayor asked, flipping pages and putting the report aside.

"A substantial increase in financial aid and support for a broad neighborhood voluntary watch group," Estelle Rives said.

The mayor picked up a pen and took notes on a yellow lined pad.

"And?"

"A special commission composed of active community members to gather information and encourage law-abiding residents to aid in ridding our area of its crime and reputation," said the third member of the group, a media favorite, the Reverend Karl Harrison.

"Right," said the mayor, writing again. He looked up at Estelle Rives. "Anything else?"

"A substantial increase in the number of African-American police officers in the area, preferably in a task force headed by an experienced African-American police officer."

"You have someone in mind," the mayor said.

"Detective Hugh Morton," said Rev. Harrison. The other two nodded their heads.

The mayor nodded and wrote the name.

"Anything else I should know before I read the report?"

"We are holding a press conference in the morning," Dr. Roland said. "If you have something of substance to have us report to the press, please let us know as soon as possible."

All three of the visitors rose and so did the mayor, who leaned over his desk to shake each of their hands.

"We would appreciate an early response to our report and requests," said Estelle Rives.

"I'll have copies made immediately and given to our people with a strongly worded request for a response by tomorrow," said the mayor. "Before your press conference."

The three visitors left. The mayor looked at his schedule. He had the parks commissioner on for four-thirty. The mayor pushed a button on the keypad by his phone and said, "Find Taradash. Get him here."

The mayor's secretary didn't answer. She didn't have to.

The mayor, into his second term, fielding problems with the skill of a seasoned second baseman, sat and looked at the report.

He knew the name of Hugh Morton. He had personally called the detective early this morning to express his sympathy for what had happened to Morton's wife. Morton had simply said, "I appreciate that." No more.

It was good politics to call the man who was probably the most visible black police officer in Chicago, but give the mayor his due, he was also outraged by what had happened and deeply moved. The mayor had been assured that an arrest was almost certain within a day. And then, a little over an hour earlier, he had received a report saying that two of the suspects in the attack on Denise Morton had been murdered and there was more than a slight chance that the man he had just been asked to appoint to a high-profile task force was a murderer.

The buzzer on his desk rang.

"Commissioner Scobiak is here," his secretary said.

"Send him in," said the mayor, sitting behind his desk and picking up his half-full cup of coffee.

He welcomed the arrival of the parks commissioner. The parks commissioner was a political hack, not terribly bright, in fear of losing his plum and always willing to say "yes" to his honor.

Scobiak was, in contrast to the three who had just left his office, an easy target. Ten minutes of browbeating the parks commissioner would do wonders for the mayor's morale.

At three minutes after four, Lieberman's grandson Barry sat down in the sanctuary at Temple Mir Shavot, opened the Scriptures to his Torah portion, flattened out the sheets of his Haftorah portion, and laid his neatly typed speech face-down on the table.

Across from him a weary-looking Rabbi Wass adjusted his glasses, nodded, and said, "Read."

Barry chanted, hoping his voice would not pick this moment to break. He lived not in fear of forgetting his portion or his speech or even of making a mistake. He lived in fear of the curse of the changing voice, the curse that had struck Michael Bernstein last year and Larry Tallent the year before.

Abe had suggested to his grandson that God may well have chosen the thirteenth year of a boy's life to have his initiation into adult Jewish responsibility for the precise reason that it was the year he was in transition.

"If it's not a trial, what does the initiation mean?" Abe had asked.

"Thirteen is the year Maori boys go alone into the bush and kill a lion," Abe had said. "At least they did when there were lions to kill. Now they probably tear up a picture of a lion."

Barry had nodded.

"A little fear and anxiety is a healthy thing," said Abe. "It helps you remember the tribulations of the rite of passage. You follow me?"

"Yes," Barry had said.

"You agree?"

"I don't know," Barry had said.

"Good," Lieberman had replied. "Go forth and multiply."

"Multiply?"

"Well," said Lieberman, "add to the number of the initiated."

And now Barry sat across from Rabbi Wass and chanted. His voice did not break. He barely looked at the pages he had been studying for months. His mind wandered and he thought about the man his grandfather had walked away with at the cemetery, the big man with the disfigured right thumb.

At three minutes after four, the phone rang at the small Chinese restaurant in the motel on Sheridan Avenue.

Iris answered. A male voice with an accent identifying him as a second-generation Chinese said, "And how will your child look?"

Iris held her breath.

"Beautiful," she said. "Who . . . ?"

"He or she will have pink Irish cheeks and red hair," the man said calmly. "Have you ever seen a Chinese with red hair?"

"I don't remember," she said. "If you intend to threaten me and my child, please do so quickly. We are about to have our first lunch customers."

"No threat," said the man. "Just something to consider. What will your aunts, uncles, cousins think? And what of your husband's family?"

"They will love my child," she said. "What do you want?"

"Nothing," the man said. "The question which I believe you have not addressed is, 'what do you want?'"

The man hung up and Iris turned to greet the three suited and laughing businessmen, lawyers, regulars, as they nodded and moved to their favorite table.

Iris carried menus to the three men, deciding that she would not tell her husband about the phone call unless, of course, others followed.

10

"You're lookin' for me," the man with the gnarled thumb said.

People were moving away from Ida Katzman's grave and toward their cars. Abe had told Bess to wait with Lisa for a few minutes. Bess had followed her husband's eyes and seen that he was staring at a heavyset man on the other side of Ida Katzman's grave. The man wore a dark suit and a properly funereal dark tie. With people moving away, the man stood alone, hands folded in front of him, feet slightly apart, eyes fixed on Abe.

"A few minutes," she had said, touching his arm. "We'll be in the car."

"Turn on the air."

"You said 'a few minutes.'"

He kissed her forehead and said, "Ten minutes. Time me."

She glanced at the big man and went to meet Lisa who stood, arms folded, waiting a few dozen feet away.

When everyone was gone, the big man slowly walked around the grave, crossed himself as he passed the hole being filled in by two men with shovels, and approached Abe.

It was then he had said, "You're lookin' for me."

"Probably," said Lieberman.

"No 'probably,'" the big man said, looking over the detective's head. "Word's out. Guy told a guy, told a guy, told me. It's this."

He held up his right hand.

"You know why I'm looking for you?"

"Something to do with a guy who got killed in New Mexico."

"Arizona, Yuma," Lieberman corrected.

"Whatever. Wherever."

"What's your name?"

"Anthony Imperioli," the man said. "No secret. You'd track it down. I'm heading whatever this shit is down before you drop it in my driveway."

The sun was in Lieberman's eyes. He moved to the right, being careful not to step on the bronze plate that marked the grave of one Seymour Glitz.

"You related to Joseph Imperioli?"

"My cousin. I'm from Boston. Moved here four, six months ago, something like that."

"Gower," said Lieberman.

"Who?"

Lieberman didn't answer.

"That the guy who got killed in, what was that, Yuma?"

"Yuma."

"I'm being honest with you, Lieberman," the man said, hands folded in front of him again. "I've been told you're a real hard-ass, which lookin' at you is a little tough to believe, but shit, I knew a guy back in Boston, Vince Falco, smaller than you, skinny like you wouldn't believe, big eyes, you know. Toughest bastard I ever knew."

"I consider it an honor to be in his company," said Lieberman. "Gower?"

"Yeah," said the big man, shifting his feet and looking down. "We're off the record here. Anything I say, I deny it later. All's we're doin' here now is talking about what a nice funeral it was."

"Gower," Lieberman repeated.

"He whacked my sister's husband two years ago. Not saying Jimmy didn't deserve it. Jimmy deserved. But he shouldn't have done it in front of my sister. He shouldn't have dragged it out, didn't have to shoot him in the goddamn eye, you know what I mean?"

"I know what you mean," said Lieberman. "Where did he do this?"

"Home. Boston. Jimmy owed big. Jimmy was into drugs, light, not heavy. Jimmy pissed some people off who it was a mistake to piss off. He threw my cousin Joe's name around a lot. Didn't do him any good."

"So you found out Gower was arrested, went to Yuma, and hired Billy Johnstone to kill him."

"Who?"

"Billy Johnstone," Lieberman repeated, checking his watch.

The man pursed his lips and shook his head.

"Never heard of him."

"He's heard of you," said Lieberman. "He described you."

"This?"

Imperioli held up his right hand.

"Jammed it in one of my old man's hunting rifles when I was a kid. Almost ripped my thumb off. Infection, operation. Damned thing almost killed me."

"And the world knows of this because . . ."

"On account of I was in the *Newsweek* magazine couple of months ago with Joe," he said. "Arms around each other. Big smiles. Family picnic. My nephew Mario got out of the army. Story mentions stuff about Joe. You know the kind of stuff. Story mentions my brother-in-law Jimmy getting hit. Think it said something about Gower being arrested, let off. Little picture of Gower, too. Black and white. Bad picture. Old. Sort of peeking around his hand."

"What were you doing in Yuma last week," Lieberman asked.

He had four more minutes.

"Never been in Yuma in my life," said Imperioli. "Swear to God. Swear to Jesus. Swear on my mother's life."

"Billy Johnstone," said Lieberman.

"Billy Johnstone. Billy Johnstone. Who the fuck is Billy Johnstone?"

"Where've you been for the last two weeks?"

"Right here," Imperioli said, emphatically pointing down at the grass. "Not right here, right here, but in Chicago right here. You can check it out. I'm settin' up a business. Construction. Got meetings every day. Contracts, dealing with permits, the whole shit. Check it out."

"I will."

"Be my guest. I'll help you."

"Got kids, Tony?"

"Three, two boys, a girl. You wanna see pictures?"

"You want to see pictures of my grandchildren?"

Neither man moved for his wallet.

"They go to college, your kids?" asked Lieberman.

"Boys graduated. Tony Junior's a lawyer. Gene's a computer something. Adrienne, she's studying literature at Grinnell. Heard of it?"

"Good school," said Lieberman.

"They say."

"Costs a lot to send kids to school."

"Where are we goin' with this?" asked Imperioli.

"You've got a lot of money, Tony?"

"Hell no," he said. "I owe my ass all over the place. If these contracts don't come through I drag my ass to my cousin Joey and hit him up for cover, which is something no one wants to do, owe Joey Imperioli money, cousin or no cousin."

"Where can I find you?" asked Lieberman.

He checked his watch. He was out of time. Tony Imperioli took out his wallet, extracted a card, and handed it to Lieberman, who looked at it. In embossed blue script it read: *Anthony Imperioli, General Contractor*. A phone number, cell phone number, and fax number were printed in smaller letters in the lower left-hand corner. There was no address. Lieberman pocketed the card.

"I'll be calling you," said Lieberman.

"Yeah. Nice funeral."

"Nice funeral," Lieberman agreed, and the two men walked together to the road where their cars were parked.

Abe got in. Bess was in the driver's seat. The air-conditioning was on and so was a classical music station.

"Mozart?" Abe asked, watching Tony Imperioli walk to a green late-model Buick and get in.

"Handel," said Lisa.

Bess started the car.

"Who was that, Abe?" Lisa asked.

"Anthony Imperioli," answered Lieberman.

"Is he a policeman, a criminal? He looks like an Italian gangster," she said as they drove past Tony Imperioli's car.

"He's a businessman," said Lieberman.

"What kind of business?" Lisa demanded.

"I'll find out," he said.

The music built to a crescendo as they passed the hill where Lieberman's parents were buried.

"Hold it," he said.

Bess stopped the car. She knew what he wanted.

"You want company?" she asked.

"No," he said. "Listen to Handel and contemplate the source of musical talent, of all talent. Genetic, accident, environment, the touch of God?"

"Abe, are you all right?" Bess asked.

"And if you solve that one," he said, patting her hand and opening the door, "contemplate the source of evil. If you come up with the same answer for both questions, let me know when I get back."

He stepped out and closed the door.

"What was that about?" Lisa asked.

Bess watched her husband move up the grassy hill between graves, heading for the spot where his parents were buried. She didn't answer her daughter.

"You think I need a haircut?" O'Neil said, looking in the rearview mirror over the dashboard and combing his hair.

"You could use one," said Hanrahan.

"Think I'll go back to the brush cut," said O'Neil, sitting back and looking at the entrance to the hospital. "You know, like Ollie North."

"Go for it," said Hanrahan behind the driver's seat.

They were waiting for Hugh Morton to come out. They could see his car parked at the corner of the hospital driveway. They knew his passenger-side visor was down displaying his police identification.

O'Neil and a plainclothes cop named Swartz had questioned the people who had gathered across from the Berg house. An old couple across the street had seen a "nice-looking Negro man" ringing the Berg doorbell a little before they heard the shots. The young mother with the child in the stroller had seen the same man get out of a white car about ten minutes before Hanrahan and O'Neil had arrived. Both the young mother and the old couple said they were pretty sure they could identify the man if they saw him again.

O'Neil had thought it would be a good idea to go right into the hospital and face Morton when he came out of his wife's room. Hanrahan had vetoed that.

"Suit yourself," said O'Neil. "But we catch him coming out of her room, he sees us, good chance he'll say something."

"He's too controlled for that."

"Hell, his wife was raped, her arm broken, his kid—"

"I know," said Bill. "We give him room, follow him when he comes out. He goes home, fine. He goes somewhere else, fine. Period."

"Period," said O'Neil.

They sat in silence. O'Neil had a Game Boy in his pocket. He pulled out the palm-sized plastic gizmo, pushed some buttons. Music began to play. Tingly, repetitive. O'Neil played Tetris.

"Can you do that without sound?" Hanrahan asked.

O'Neil turned off the sound and kept pushing buttons.

"Keeps me calm," said O'Neil. "Helps pass the time."

"Here he comes," said Bill.

O'Neil hit a button to pause the game and looked up. Morton was heading quickly to his car, a white Honda.

"Slick-looking nigger," said O'Neil with what sounded like genuine admiration.

"Cut that shit," said Hanrahan, starting the engine.

"What?"

"That 'nigger' shit," said Hanrahan. "Your wife was—"

"The man's good," O'Neil cut in. "I'm on his side. If he

killed those two weasel scumbags, I hope he gets away with it. I'll kick in twenty bucks to buy him a goddamn medal. How's that?"

They followed Morton slowly, carefully.

"Perfect," said Hanrahan.

O'Neil turned the game off and tucked it into his jacket pocket.

"Don't like me much, do you?" he said.

"Seen worse," Hanrahan said, eyes front.

"Rather be with the little Jew than a fellow mick?"

"Much," said Hanrahan.

"Then let's nail this down so you can go sit with him and drink *mattie* ball soup on Devon."

"Suits me," said Bill.

"I have that fuckin' effect on people," O'Neil said with a sigh.

"Makes you wonder, doesn't it?" asked Hanrahan.

Rabbi Wass's office wasn't too small for the gathering but Irving Hammel decided that they should move to the conference room where he could roam as he spoke. The room had a table, eight chairs, and reproductions of Chagall paintings on the wall. Through the window one could watch the traffic on Dempster.

Bess and Abe sat together. Rabbi Wass sat next to them, and Irving, standing on the opposite side of the table, solemnly removed papers from his attaché case and laid them in two neat piles before him.

"I have six copies of Ida Katzman's will," he said, pointing to one of the piles.

Lieberman tried to pay attention. His thoughts flitted from an old black man in a Yuma hospital, to two very sweet and aggressive old women who were planning Barry's bar mitzvah and expecting a payment within a few days, to Lisa who desperately wanted wisdom from him so that she could scornfully reject it.

"Before I pass them out, in accordance with Mrs. Katzman's wishes, I'll state simply what the conditions of the will are."

He paused pregnantly, dramatically, and adjusted his glasses.

"Read the will, Marc Anthony," Lieberman said wearily.

"Abe," Bess said with a tolerant sigh, which stated clearly that one could expect no more from her husband.

"Forty thousand dollars to the United Negro College Fund," he said looking at the will. "Another forty thousand to Hadassah. One hundred and ten thousand dollars to her driver and companion, Mr. Arthur Burke. One million six hundred dollars to Temple Mir Shavot to be applied according to the wishes of the temple board."

Hammel removed his glasses dramatically, looked up and said, "There is a proviso. It was Mrs. Katzman's preference that the money be invested and that only the annual interest be applied to the temple's needs unless there was a crisis, which required touching the capital. A crisis would be defined by Rabbi Wass or whoever the rabbi might be and the president of the congregation."

Hammel looked down at the will again and read, "The endowment is not to bear my name. There are to be no plaques bearing my name. I do not want someone forty or fifty years from now to see my name and wonder who this person of the past might be, or worse, to not wonder. I care only to be remembered by those still living. And so I wish that those present at the end of the reading of this will recite the mourner's Kaddish."

No one spoke. All nodded.

"Finally, there is sixty thousand dollars that will go to Bess

Lieberman," he said. "Mrs. Lieberman is expressly asked to spend the money on her own needs and that of her family."

Hammel handed out copies of the will and said, "As you will see, I am to serve as executor of the estate at an annual fee of twenty thousand dollars. Any questions?"

"Who gets her cane?" asked Lieberman.

"Her cane?" asked Hammel.

"Yes, her cane," Lieberman repeated.

"It's not in the will," said Hammel.

"I'd like it," said Lieberman.

"But . . . ," Hammel said.

"Yes," said Rabbi Wass. "Take the cane, Abraham."

"Thank you," said Lieberman.

"If there are no more questions," said Hammel.

"There is nothing in the will that forbids us to have a memorial light in her honor?" asked Rabbi Wass.

"Nothing."

"Good," said Rabbi Wass. "And now let us honor Ida Katzman's wish and recite the mourner's Kaddish."

There was no need for a prayer book. All four of the people in the room had said the words since childhood in honor of the memory of mothers, fathers, husbands, wives, brothers, sisters, aunts, uncles, friends, and even children.

Rabbi Wass began in Hebrew, "Magnified and sanctified be the great name of God, in the world created according to the Divine will. May God's sovereignty soon be established. In our lifetime and that of the entire house of Israel. And let us say . . ."

And the four said "Amen" and continued in Hebrew:

"Y'hey sh'mey raba m'varah l'alamul-almey alma-ya. May God's great name be praised to all eternity."

They completed the prayer in unison in Hebrew, "Hallowed and honored, extolled and exalted, adored and acclaimed be the name of the blessed Holy One, whose glory is above all the praises, hymns, and songs of adoration which human beings can utter. And let us say, Amen.

"May God grant abundant peace and life to us and to all Israel. And let us say, Amen.

"May God, who ordains harmony in the universe, grant peace to us and to all Israel. And let us say: Amen."

Back in the car Abe said, "We didn't say the meditation before the Kaddish."

"She didn't ask for it," said Bess.

"There's nothing in the Kaddish about death or grief," said Lieberman.

"It's not a prayer of grief," she said. "It's a—"

"Meditation," he finished.

They were silent for the next two blocks and then Bess spoke.

"She wanted us to enjoy the money."

"Yeah," said Lieberman, making the turn onto Jarvis.

"What do we need, Abe?"

"We'll have no trouble thinking of something," he said, parking the car in a space across from their house.

"The cane," she said as they sat, not wanting to get out.

"I liked Ida," he said.

"I know. I still think we should put it on the wall in the living room," she said.

"I still think it could go into the front closet," he said.

"Yes, I know. Where one or both of us could use it when we got old enough to need it. Getting it down from the wall wouldn't be all that difficult," said Bess, patting his arm. "Look."

She was looking at a little red Kia parked a few spaces down and across the street.

"I see it," he said.

The sisters were here for the final bar mitzvah arrangements. Lieberman wondered how long it would take for Ida Katzman's bequest to be available so they could finish paying for the bar mitzvah.

Lieberman's cell phone rang as Bess opened her door.

"Lieberman," he said and then listened. Bess saw that whoever was speaking had Abe's full attention. He touched his thumb to his mustache. This, Bess knew, was a bad sign. "Doesn't give me much time," he said to the caller. "I'll be there."

He pushed the button, turning off the phone, and looked at his wife.

"You'll have to face the sisters Karamazov on your own," he said.

"You should take something to eat," Bess said.

"I'm going to a restaurant," he said. "We're rich now, remember?"

"Abe, you've got that look."

"Which one?"

"Lean and hungry and something on your mind," she said.

"All three correct," he said.

"Be careful," she said.

"Aren't I always?"

"No," she said.

"I'll be careful," he said.

Bess moved toward the front door and watched him go to the car and pull away.

He had, if the caller was right, about an hour. Abe patted his gun and considered what he might have time to eat before hell froze over.

There was something scary about the gun.

Blue walked, head down, feeling the weight in his pocket.

He had no intention of using it, but he had decided there in the living room of his house as he fired, that he would not throw it away. He walked.

Where the hell was he walking? He needed a plan, but nothing came, not even the germ of an idea. He was hungry. He had spent three dollars and change for the Big Mac and chicken sandwich special, but he was still hungry.

It dawned on him slowly as he walked, so slowly that he didn't recognize it when it came. It was just there. He had walked right past it and then it had caught up with him. He had just taken the gun and run. No thought, just take it and get the hell away.

He had run because he was scared, the bodies of Easy Dan and Comedy lying there, the cops at the door. A gun would be a good thing to have. He had taken it and run.

But now Blue had a mission, a meaning in life, something he had to do, a damn good deed. He had someone who needed his help.

Why hadn't he recognized it before? He had just done what he had done without thinking about it, but something inside him had made him do it, made him do it for someone else.

He would have done it for Comedy or Easy Dan but that was different.

He kept walking and thinking and not noticing the police cruiser that had begun following him.

The two members of the Twin Dragons inside the Vietnamese restaurant on Argyle were seated in the rear, in a booth, in near darkness. The two young women with them were giggling and finishing green-tea ice cream, which they ate with very small spoons.

There had been music playing when they came in almost an hour earlier, but the music had stopped now.

At a booth in front of the same restaurant watching the two Chinese couples were four young men speaking Spanish quietly.

Across the street in a black car with tinted windows sat four Chinese men with guns in their laps watching the four Puerto Ricans watching the two couples.

And then five things happened at once.

The Twin Dragons got out of their car.

The four Puerto Ricans reached for the guns in their pockets.

The two young Chinese men in the booth motioned to the young women across from them to get on the floor.

The door to the kitchen of the restaurant flew open and two Chinese men with automatic weapons stepped out.

And Abe Lieberman and Mr. Woo, who had been sitting in another booth drinking tea, stood up.

Woo looked at the Chinese men in the booth, in front of the kitchen, and coming through the door. They froze. Abe looked at the Puerto Ricans, held up his cell phone, and said, "Which one of you is Hernandez?"

The tallest of the surrounded quartet of Puerto Ricans took a quick breath.

Lieberman held out his phone and said, "El Perro would like a word with you."

11

"You're doing what you have to do," Hugh Morton said after letting O'Neil and Hanrahan into his house in spite of his sister-in-law's initial arms-folded barring of the door.

He had known they followed him home from the hospital. He was upset, probably not thinking quite straight, but he had known the two policemen had followed him. Morton was a good cop, twenty years–plus experience. He had been the one doing the following more times then he could remember and the two men in front of him had not been difficult to spot.

The sister-in-law disappeared as Morton ushered the detectives into a kitchen on the other side of a reasonably spacious living room–dining room. The table was bright blond wood, the chairs matched. The coffee in the Braun machine tucked in a corner of the counter next to the double sink filled the room with the smell of a tinctured berry.

Morton motioned to the chairs. The two men sat.

"Coffee?"

"Yes," said Hanrahan.

"Sure," said O'Neil.

"Cream?"

"Yes," said Hanrahan.

"Black," said O'Neil, meeting Morton's eyes with a very small smile.

"We've got witnesses," said Hanrahan.

"To what?" asked Morton, pouring the coffee into yellow mugs with smiling faces on the side of each.

"You were on North Rockwell a few hours ago," said Hanrahan.

"I was on North Rockwell," said Morton, placing a steaming mug in front of each of them.

He went back and poured himself one, too.

"Black, like you," he said, raising his mug in a toast to O'Neil.

O'Neil returned the toast.

"You want a lawyer?" Hanrahan asked.

"Not yet," said Morton, sitting. "I was there. Tracked Berg. It wasn't hard. I read your report, went to the burger place."

He shrugged and drank.

"Old woman saw you," said O'Neil. "The kid's grandmother."

"Saw me?"

"Saw you shoot Berg and the other kid," said O'Neil.

"They weren't kids," said Morton, biting his lower lip. "And she didn't see me shoot them because I didn't shoot them."

A boy, about five, stepped into the kitchen. He wore a red Chicago Bulls T-shirt with a snorting bull on the front. The boy looked frightened. He was the coffee color of his father but there was a leanness and a doe-eyed look that must have come from his mother.

"You didn't come up," the boy said, moving to his father's side.

"Just got here," Morton said. "These men looked like they needed some coffee."

"You policemen?" the boy asked.

"We are," said Hanrahan.

"You got the people who hurt my mom?"

"Looks that way," said Hanrahan.

"Are they dead?"

"Looks that way," Hanrahan repeated.

"Good," said the boy. "Did *you* kill them?"

"No," said O'Neil, looking at Morton, who hugged his son to his side.

"Want some coffee?" Morton asked the boy.

"Huh?"

"Special treat," said Morton. "Bring the milk."

The boy got a mug and a plastic carton of milk. Morton poured some milk into the cup and added a little coffee and two spoons of sugar. He stirred it and handed it to his son.

"Hughie, these men are Detectives Hanrahan and O'Neil," Morton said.

The boy nodded.

"You take your coffee up to your room. I've got some police business to talk to the detectives about. I'll be up when we finish."

"Aunt Dee says Mom is doing okay," he said. "Maybe I can see her."

"Maybe," said Morton. "We'll talk later."

Hughie held the mug in both hands as he left the room, careful not to spill.

"Nice kid," said Hanrahan.

"I didn't kill them," said Morton. "I went to the house. The car with the monkey dangling from the rearview was parked in front. I looked through the windows. The curtains were thick but I could see people in there."

"And you walked in and started shooting, but one of them got away," said O'Neil.

"No. I was this close," Morton said, looking at the doorway to be sure his son wasn't there and holding his thumb and finger about an inch apart.

"And?" Hanrahan prompted, working on his coffee.

"And," Morton said, "I decided to go see my wife."

"Just leave them there?" O'Neil said.

"I knew where to find them," said Morton, meeting O'Neil's eyes. "If I went in and blew them away, I'd lose my wife, my son. They need me. I need them."

"And the third one?" asked O'Neil.

"And the old woman?" asked Hanrahan.

"Didn't see them," said Morton after taking a sip of coffee. "Must have been in another room."

"Simple as that?" asked O'Neil.

"Simple as that," said Morton. "I knew you were maybe ten, fifteen minutes behind me. I didn't want to be there when you showed up."

"You left the scene of a crime," said O'Neil.

Morton nodded and drank some more coffee.

"Went straight to the hospital?" asked Hanrahan.

"Stopped at St. Stephen's Church," Morton said. "It didn't do any good. Five minutes, no more. Then the hospital."

"Your piece," said O'Neil. "Mind if we check it?"

Morton nodded, reached under his jacket, and handed his weapon across the table. O'Neil took it, examined it, and handed it back.

"Have a backup?" asked O'Neil.

"No," said Morton. "You didn't find the gun?"

"Can we have the lab check your hands or do you want that lawyer now?" asked Hanrahan.

Morton looked at his watch.

"Let's make it quick," he said, getting up. "I've got an important dinner meeting."

O'Neil and Hanrahan stood.

"Mind if we ask who this important dinner meeting's with?" said O'Neil.

"The mayor," said Morton, taking the empty mug from O'Neil's hand.

Abe was certain that when he got home a few minutes after ten, the Pinchuk sisters would be long gone. He had not even considered the possibility that they would be there, which proved, as Bess often said, that while her husband seemed to be ever prepared for the unexpected in his life as a police officer, he was never prepared for the expected in his personal life.

Here, before him at his dining room table, sat living proof that Bess was right.

Everyone called them "the Pinchuk girls" though Rose was seventy-six and Esther seventy-five. They were both widows. They lived together. They wore each other's clothes and could have passed for twins. The Pinchuk girls were short, looked deceptively frail, wore identical short haircuts for their identical silver hair, and bore the same face as their late mother, which meant they were unblemished and perpetually smiling as if they had a secret and knew how to tolerate even the most outrageous responses the world hurled at them. They were thin, female Jewish Buddhas who sat smiling up at him with large ring-bound books laid out and piled ponderously on each other.

"Ladies," Abe said, wanting to take off his shoes and kick them into the front closet, but that would result in the mild but certain disapproval of his wife when the visitors had left. "I'm sorry I'm late."

"Listen," said Esther. "If it can't be helped, it can't be helped."

"I was preventing a gang war," Abe said, deciding to keep his jacket on to cover his holster and gun.

"A gang war?" asked Rose. "Coloreds?"

"Yes, but not the color you're thinking of," said Abe as he sat.

"Guns?" asked Esther.

"A plethora," said Lieberman, reaching for one of the chocolate chip cookies on a plate within reach. "A cornucopia of firearms."

"Is he joking, Bess?" asked Rose. "I can't tell when he's joking."

"I don't know," said Bess. "Abe, are you joking?"

"No."

"He's not joking," said Bess. "My husband enjoys displaying his vocabulary."

"I read a lot," said Abe, reaching for a second cookie.

Bess held her hand out and her husband reluctantly dropped the cookie onto her palm.

"Insomnia," said Lieberman. "Can't sleep so I read. Amazing what the mind can retain when you're so tired you have no idea what you are reading."

"Never mind," said Esther, raising her tiny hands. "We don't need to hear."

"Abraham," Rose said, a distinct note of excitement in her voice. "We're ready."

"Three days," said Esther.

"The big day is in three days," Rose agreed. "Responses are all in. Catering is all set. Friday night *Oneg* at the temple is cake, *ruggalah*, petits fours, decaffeinated coffee, and tea."

"And sugar-free cookies," added Esther.

"And sugar-free cookies," agreed Rose.

Abe looked at Bess, who sat at his side as Esther passed an open book to him.

"That's how it will look."

"Wonderful," said Lieberman.

"And the buffet lunch on Saturday," Esther said, reaching over to point to a photograph on the next page. "Tuna salad, egg salad, herring, bagels and lox spread, and a nice green salad."

"And fruit salad," said Rose.

"And cookies," Esther added.

Lieberman examined the photographs.

"You have our gratitude," Lieberman said.

"Bimah flowers from Hoisman's on Skokie Boulevard," said Rose, turning the page and pointing to a photograph of flowers.

"It's perfect," said Bess.

"The flowers were paid for by Ida Katzman weeks ago," said Esther.

"We know," said Lieberman.

"Doesn't hurt to remind," said Rose. "Rabbi Wass will mention. You might want to mention, too, when you talk."

That left only the bar mitzvah–night dinner, a sore topic with the Pinchuk girls. Maish and Yetta had insisted on catering and paying, which meant it would be kosher style and not kosher. This was fine with Bess and Abe and even with Rabbi Wass, but not with the Pinchuks, who accepted the fact stoically. They would have preferred Feinstein and

Brinkoff and they would have preferred the hall at Temple Mir Shavot and not the private dining room of the Jewish War Veterans' building in Lincolnwood.

"Boxes of yarmulkes will be inside the shul door both Friday and Saturday," said Rose.

"Blue and white, like you wanted," said Esther.

"It's what Barry wanted," said Lieberman.

"They look nice," said Rose tolerantly.

"Mrs. Lieberman has the 'thank you' notes and envelopes," said Esther, pointing to a white box in front of Bess.

"And all that remains is for us to give you our sincere thanks and a final check for your tireless efforts," said Abe.

The Pinchuk girls smiled.

"I gave the ladies a check," said Bess.

Abe nodded.

"We heard from sources that Ida Katzman left you a million dollars," said Rose.

"Your sources have active imaginations," said Abe. "And the money was left to Mrs. Lieberman."

"I'm sure you will make a generous *tzadakeh* gift," said Rose.

"It will go to those who have need for it," said Bess.

"So," said Rose with a sigh. "I suppose now we fold our books like Arabs and silently steal away."

"And the night shall be filled with music," Lieberman began. "And the cares that infest the day shall fold their tents like Arabs and silently steal away."

"Shakespeare?" asked Esther, obviously impressed.

"Longfellow," said Lieberman.

"Insomnia?"

"Insomnia," Lieberman confirmed. "A blessing and a curse."

"One of God's mysteries," said Rose.

"Thanks again," said Bess, standing and helping them place their books in the worn leather bag they had brought with them. "You'll be there for everything?"

"Would we miss it?" asked Rose.

"Dinner at the Jewish War Veterans'?" asked Lieberman.

"We will be in attendance," said Esther.

Abe and Bess ushered the Pinchuks to the door and helped them to their car.

"Rose has to drive," said Esther. "My night vision is not good. Rose inherited our grandmother Sarah's vision. Died at ninety-nine, never needed glasses. Me, I got our father's eyes."

"It evens out," Abe said, closing the door after she was inside.

And then they were gone.

"We have anything left in the checking?" he asked Bess as they went back to the house.

"You get paid Friday," she said. "We can get a bank loan based on Ida's will. I checked."

"We'll talk about it tomorrow," he said as they entered the house and he closed the door. "Kids sleeping?"

"I'll check," she said.

"Lisa?"

"She wanted to talk to you. I asked her to wait till tomorrow. Told her you were busy saving the world. You know what she said?"

"She said, 'Again.'"

"That's exactly what she said," said Bess, moving to clear the dinning room table.

"And?"

"She said it's easier for you to save the world than to save your only daughter," said Bess. "Was it really a gang war, Avrum?"

"It was," he said, taking off his jacket. "A potential gang war. Chinese and Puerto Ricans."

He followed Bess into the kitchen.

"Abe, tell me, are there really Jewish gangs?"

"There are," he said. "Jamaican, Hungarian, Russian, Irish, Indonesian, Mexican. We live in a land of unlimited opportunity."

"You ate?"

"I did," he said. "Vietnamese ribs and noodle soup."

"And that sweet coffee?" she asked.

"It would have been impolite to do anything else," he said. "And I was with a man who values politeness."

Even, thought Lieberman, when he is setting up the fall of people who trust him. He had no intention of telling Bess what had happened. She had no desire to hear it. It would have been a tough tale to tell had she been interested.

Woo had an informant in the Twin Dragons, an informant who told him about the plan to ambush the Puerto Ricans. Woo did not want a street war, did not want the television stations and newspapers to put Chinese names and faces in front of the public, perhaps even his own name and face. It had happened before and he did not want it to happen again.

It was not that Woo was a stranger to violence, gang war, and murder. He had risen to his present position largely because he had employed such tools. But having attained, he now wanted to retain and enjoy the privilege, artifacts, and respect of old age.

Woo had informed Lieberman than Parker Liao in his ambition and lack of conscience might well present to the city a spectacle of such carnage that the minor street brawls of old tongs and those of the Mafia would be forever relegated to ancient and quaint history.

A battle with a gang of Puerto Ricans led by a madman was not such a necessity. Hence, he had called Lieberman. Parker Liao was definitely a threat and a liability—one that Mr. Woo preferred to deal with later and quietly.

There was no talking to the Puerto Ricans and their madman leader, Woo had said. That he would leave to Lieberman. He would, however, reluctantly add his presence to the planned site of carnage to defuse the situation. It would be Lieberman's job to keep the incident from the public eye and to arrange, with Woo's support, a truce, a cease-fire, perhaps even a meeting.

The meeting was scheduled, if possible, to take place the next day. Lieberman didn't put much hope in such a get-together. He had seen El Perro and Parker Liao face each other on the street.

Bess turned out the downstairs lights, leaving only the night-light in the bathroom and the light over the sink in the kitchen.

Abe and Bess moved to their bedroom on the first floor beyond the dining room. The stairs leading to the children's rooms was outside their door. Lisa was doubling up with her daughter, and Barry, three days from officially being a man in the eyes of God, was in his own room.

Lieberman removed his gun and holster, placed them in the drawer of the night table on his side of the bed, and locked the drawer with the key he wore around his neck.

Bess moved to the closet.

"A long day," she said, taking off her dress.

"A long day," Abe agreed, sitting on the bed to take off his trousers.

"You're going to try to sleep?" she said, removing her slip.

"I'll take a bath, read a little," he said, folding his trousers.

"Why not try the pills Dr. Feinberg gave you to sleep?"

The reasons why he did not take the pills were convoluted and not completely known to Abraham Lieberman. He said he didn't like the idea of being helpless and sedated. Another reason supported his insomnia. He had a love-hate relationship with his affliction. He was frequently tired from too little sleep, but he was also comfortable in his late-night fatigue, the solitary time in the hot water of a bath reading whatever he had accumulated, or sitting in the living room in front of the television watching black-and-white movies he had seen years before and often since. His insomnia was his alone, his comforting partner, and his enemy.

When they were in their pajamas, Lieberman kissed his wife, said "good night," and turned off the light. A heavy weariness settled on him and he considered actually trying to sleep, an attempt that usually left him frustrated.

This time the weariness brought to mind Billy Johnstone in a hospital bed in Yuma, Arizona. Lieberman lay back, closed his eyes, and fell asleep. The old man in the bed in Yuma winked at him.

12

Between the time Abe went to sleep a few minutes before three in the morning and was awakened by the humming of his alarm clock at six, the following had taken place inside the city limits of Chicago:

A twenty-two-year-old named Daryl McCracken, who had moved to the city from Dry Oak, Tennessee, five months earlier, was beaten to death by Simon Pardee, fifty-three, the boyfriend of Daryl's mother. All three had been drinking in the mother's house in the Lakeview District. They got into an argument over Daryl's lack of employment and the fact that Simon paid all the bills. Simon used his fists. Daryl's mother, Martha Ann, was too drunk to remember any of it.

Mario Stancini, a twenty-one-year veteran of the Chicago police department, was shot to death by seventy-seven-year-old Martin Terwiliger while serving a subpoena for Terwiliger to appear in housing court. Terwiliger's two-flat apartment building just off of Cicero Avenue near Midway Airport was in serious need of repair. Sancini was assigned to District 17 but was "detailed" to the Corporation Council's Office. District 17 had been overloaded and Stancini's detailing was considered to be a few weeks of easy duty.

Arida Royce, thirty, killed her boyfriend and the father of their two children, ages six and four, in their apartment in a public housing complex on Roosevelt Road. She claimed he was angry because she came home at two in the morning after working a double shift at an all-night Wendy's nearby on Jackson just outside the Loop. She claimed he threatened her. She claimed it was self-defense. The boyfriend was found in bed and appeared to have been sleeping. She had hit him in the head fifteen times with a baseball bat. He had been out of jail for one week for a drug conviction and had been found not guilty on two counts of homicide the year before. The state's attorney had no intention of pursuing the circumstances of the death.

At two in the morning, a seventeen-year-old girl and a sixteen-year-old girl were shot in the 8000 block of South Woodlawn in the South Shore District south of the University of Chicago. Both were shot once in the back when someone started to shoot into a group of teens congregated in front of an all-night liquor store. The seventeen-year-old died. The sixteen-year-old was alive and being treated in Christ Hospital. The seventeen-year-old had a one-year-old daughter. In three days, the police would find and arrest two men who said they had been shooting at two men the girls had been talking to. The four men had been in a bar fight two hours earlier. Neither the dead girl nor the one who survived had been in the bar.

Hope Simmon, seventy-five, was shot in the head just after midnight in a home invasion on the South Side. Hope and her eighty-four-year-old brother sold candy from her apartment in a housing project. Everyone in the project knew it, including Roy Tomkins, sixteen, who forced his way into her apartment wearing a mask. Hope recognized him, addressed him by name. Tomkins fired, grabbed thirty-seven dollars and a box of M&M's, Junior Mints, and Toot-sie Rolls, and left forgetting to shoot the weeping brother. The police went to Tomkins's home. Easy to find. Mask and gun in the garage. He had robbed the Simmon apartment eight months earlier. That time he got away with forty-two dollars and four Snickers bars.

At the furthest edge of the city almost into Calumet, there was a three-way shoot-out between the Latin Dragons, the Latin Counts, and the Latin Kings. Someone was on the wrong turf. The only one hit by a bullet was a city bus driver named Leroy Vanescuva who was asleep in bed when the stray shot went through his first-floor bedroom window. The bullet took off the little finger on his left hand. It was the fifth exchange of gunfire between the three gangs in the last six days. They had taken Sunday off out of respect for their parents.

James Murray Bendner, thirty-two, a Gangster Disciple, released from prison one day earlier after serving three years on a drug charge, was shot at one-fifteen in the morning inside a home he was visiting. Two males in hoods and masks invaded the home and shot Bendner six times. There were ten witnesses. It was a known crack house. On their way out, the perpetrators robbed and pistol-whipped a man sitting in front of the house who said the shooters were Black Gangster Disciples. Ten minutes later the injured man changed his mind.

At two in the morning, an unidentified man randomly shot two people on Hollywood Avenue on the North Side. The shooter drove a fenderless old Chevy to a nearby motel. The hostage barricade terrorist team hit the killer's room and found the man dead of a self-inflicted gunshot wound to the head. There was no identification in his pockets or in the room and he had registered as Thomas Aquinas.

Just after midnight, Paul Berg, known as Blue by the few friends he had, a number that had been reduced by two the day before with the shooting death of Comedy and Easy Dan, was arrested by two uniformed officers as he lay on a bench at a bus stop at the corner of Lawrence and Broadway. He gave them no trouble and withdrew the gun from his pocket with thumb and finger as he was told.

He laid the gun down gently on the bench as both officers leveled their weapons at him. Before six in the morning, the gun would definitely be identified as the one that had killed Comedy and Easy Dan.

At five A.M. the phone in Iris and Bill Hanrahan's bedroom rang. The dog sleeping near the door woke up and Bill, sitting up, could see its green eyes looking at him. Bill picked up the phone on the third ring. He was used to calls in the middle of the night. He was a cop.

"Got the guy with the gun, one that killed those two on Rockwell," came the weary voice of Detective Stan Green. "Want to come in?"

"Be there in an hour," Bill said, hanging up and swinging his legs over the side of the bed.

He was aware of Iris sitting up beside him, her hand resting on his shoulder. He reached back to pat her hand reassuringly. The dog ambled to the bed. Bill touched its head.

"Got to get up," he said.

He had started to rise when the phone rang again. He picked it up.

"Yeah, Stan," he said.

"Is your wife awake?" came the soft voice of what

sounded like a young man. The words were precise and distinctly articulated.

"Who is this?" Bill asked.

"A person calling from a phone in the lobby of the Drake Hotel," he answered.

"What do you want with her?" Hanrahan said.

"I'd prefer to tell her. Just say it is the concerned individual who spoke to her earlier about the difficulties certain children face when they are brought into the world by parents who have not considered the consequences of their actions."

"Why don't you just tell me," Bill said, looking back at Iris, who had turned on the light on the table near her side of the bed.

"Very well," said the man amiably. "The child she will bear, if you allow that to happen, will be a mongrel, perhaps a fair and even handsome or beautiful mongrel, but a mongrel nonetheless. It is not a good idea to have a child who will have to face the scorn of two hostile cultures. And there are far greater consequences. I tell you this as a friend."

"Well, friend," said Bill, forcing himself to be as amiable as the caller. "You are a little squeal of a bastard. I intend to find you and do you some much-deserved bodily harm."

"I'll call again," the man said. "This seems to be a bad time."

He hung up. Bill pressed *99 and waited while the phone rang. He let it ring, reaching back to take Iris's hand. It rang six times, seven times, eight times. And then someone said, "Yeah?"

"Who are you?" asked Hanrahan.

"Who am . . . I'm a person on the way up to my room from the bar is who I am. Who are you?"

The man sounded mildly drunk.

"The police," said Bill. "Did you see a man walking away from this phone?"

"A . . . only other person I see is a guy walking across the lobby. It's I-don't-know-what-time-in-the-morning. Not many people wandering around."

"Describe him," said Hanrahan.

"The guy walking across the lobby?"

"Yeah."

"I don't know. About thirty maybe, maybe more. Nice sport jacket. His back's to me. Dark hair. He's turning a little, looking back at me."

There was a pause.

"What's going on?" asked Bill.

"I'm waving to him to come back," the man said. "You want to talk to him, right?"

"Is he coming?"

"No, but he smiled. He's leaving the hotel now."

"Would you recognize him if you saw him again?" asked Bill.

"Don't think so, but maybe. Did I tell you my name?"

"What's your name?"

"Sorry," said the man. "I'm not getting involved in whatever this is. I'm hanging up and going to my room."

"Wait," said Hanrahan.

"Oh," said the man. "The guy in the lobby. He's Chinese, Japanese, something like that."

The man hung up. So did Bill.

"Don't answer the phone," he said to Iris. "I'll call and have the number changed. You know who that was?"

"A person who called me earlier," she said. "I didn't want you to know."

"Our phone number's not listed," he said.

"It doesn't matter," Iris said. "I know who the caller is. I recognized his voice."

Abe showered, shampooed, shaved, dressed, got his gun out of the night-table drawer, and kissed his wife. Bess opened her eyes.

"Good morning," he said.

"That's a kiss?" she said.

He kissed her again, this time with what started as a desire to please her that turned into a desire to please himself.

"Hold that thought, Lieberman," she said.

"Maybe we can get to bed early tonight," he said. "I can always get up later if I can't sleep."

"Something to look forward to," she said. "I'm going back to sleep."

He carried his shoes in his left hand, closed the bedroom door behind him, and went silently in his socks to the kitchen to microwave a cup of coffee in his small Starbucks thermos cup before heading to the T&L, where he would savor a lox and onion omelet before heading for the station.

He opened the kitchen door. Lisa was sitting in her white terry cloth robe, a cup of coffee nested in her two hands.

"You know where I got this robe?" she asked.

"Your mother and I gave it to you when you were sixteen," he said, moving to the rack near the sink where his thermos sat. "We got it from a hotel in New York where we went to your cousin Sol's wedding. It's got *Taft Hotel* written on the back. It's been hanging at the back of your closet for more than ten years."

"You stole it from the hotel," said Lisa.

Lieberman scratched his chin.

"No," he said. "We paid for it as a gift for you. All this time you thought we stole it?"

"I'm not sure I believe you," she said.

Lieberman poured himself some of yesterday's coffee from the glass pot nestled into the machine near the microwave.

"Ask your mother," he said. "You got up to accuse me of a ten-year-old misdemeanor?"

"Almost fifteen years old," she said. "And that's not why I'm up. Couldn't sleep. I think I've got your insomnia."

Another item on my daughter's list of grievances against her father, Lieberman thought.

Lieberman filled the thermos with the remainder of yesterday's coffee, put the thermos into the microwave, set it for one minute, and pushed the start button. He turned to face his daughter while it hummed away.

"He's coming," she said.

"The Messiah?" he asked blandly.

"That's not funny, Abe."

"It's early in the morning. Who's coming?"

"My husband," she said. "He'll be here this afternoon. He wants me to come back. God knows why."

"You sure God knows why? You ever wonder how God stores all this information?" he said. "Or why?"

"Abe."

"Sorry, bad night and I've got some things that are going to make it a bad day. And I have a headache. And my stomach . . ."

"What am I going to do?" Lisa asked, looking at him for an answer she would almost certainly ignore in favor of whatever one was dwelling inside her ready to pop out when she gave it half a chance.

The microwave *binged* to let him know his coffee was ready.

"I like him," Lieberman said.

"And me?"

"You I love."

"Why?"

"Why?" he repeated. "You're my only child. You are half a lifetime of memories that give meaning to my existence. You are the mother of my beloved grandchildren. When I look at you I pray to whatever God or Gods may be that nothing happens to you."

"Do you like me?" she asked earnestly.

"Most of the time," he said. "About seventy-five percent. The question, however, is 'Do you like me?'"

"I love you, Abe," she said.

"Give me a 'like' percentage," he said, taking the thermos out of the microwave and pressing on the top.

"Fifty?" she said.

"An improvement over the last time," he said. "Progress."

"I asked you for advice," she said.

He walked over to her, thermos in his left hand, and put out his right to touch his daughter's cheek. She didn't turn away.

"Stop being angry at yourself," he said. "Whatever you've done wrong is in the past. And not everything you've done is wrong. And you've got a lot of years to do what's right."

"Yeah," she said, smiling.

It wasn't much of a smile but it was real.

"And," he added, "if you stop being angry at yourself, I can hope you'll stop being angry at me for my countless parental misdeeds."

"I think I'll go back to sleep," she said. "The kids will be up in a few hours."

"Your mother will get them to school," he said.

"I think I'll let her sleep."

There was nothing more to say. Not at the moment. Lieberman left the house.

"This is the day," Wayne said aloud as he lay in bed and watched the gray twi-morning turn to sunny bright.

Definitely today. He would shower, shave, spend a little time carefully deciding what to wear, have breakfast out. Yes, definitely. This was an important day, the day he would kill Lee Cole Carter.

He wanted to see people, let them know how he felt, how important he felt, how alive he felt. He had been alone too long. Well, not actually alone. He had people he knew, people he did signs for, people he got his haircuts from, but not people to sit across from in his own kitchen in the morning and talk about what was in the *Tribune* or what was on *Good Morning America*.

Maybe, if he lived, just maybe, he would get to meet Charlie Gibson and Diane Sawyer. He would be on the show, sitting in one of those comfortable-looking chairs, and they would be sympathetic. They would try to understand. And when he was off he would watch them commenting on the interview.

Maybe Diane would say, "A heartbreaking story."

And Charlie would answer, "And he seems so upbeat, likable."

No, it would not be live. It would have to be a remote, probably from the jail. There was no way they would let him go to New York to be on *Good Morning America*.

When his father died, Wayne had been given a cat by Sam Vigroner at the Master Cleaner's. He had tried to love the cat, talk to it, but it was just a cat, which reminded him that he had no person to talk to, laugh with. The cat didn't laugh or smile or understand. It wasn't that he didn't like the cat. He just didn't like the idea of people . . . He didn't like people saying, "There goes Wayne Czerbiak, the one with the cat."

And so he had given the cat, fully neutered, all shots given, several months' supply of food, a litter box, and a big sack of Tidy Cat to Blanche Olesnanik across the street. Blanche was old, maybe eighty, bent over with arthritis. She had welcomed the cat when Wayne said he would come over every three days to feed it, change the food and the water and the litter and that he would pay for everything.

"I just want him to have a good home," he had told her.

"Won't you miss him?" Blanche had said.

He wouldn't, but he said, with his trademark grin, "I'll come and visit, remember."

And that had been that. He had returned to Blanche's every three days right on schedule except for the time that he had the flu and didn't want to give it to her. Whenever he visited, Blanche had root beer and Toll House cookies and when he remembered he said something appropriate about the cat, which she had named "Winkie."

On one of these visits it occurred to Wayne that he had never given the cat a name.

That was past. Blanche would probably have to take care of the cat on her own. He placed two hundred dollars in twenty-dollar bills in an envelope, addressed the envelope to Blanche, put a stamp on the envelope, and inserted a note in a perfect calligraphic script saying, "This is to take care of Winkie."

Wayne was a realist.

He had put on a pair of clean jeans, a white shirt, and a colorful tie with guitars floating on it in a white cloud-filled sky.

Then Wayne had checked his father's gun to be sure it was properly loaded before tucking it into the pocket of his Lakeview High School jacket.

Gun in pocket, letter to Blanche in hand, Wayne left the house locking it and headed down the street for Rosie's four blocks away.

He was most assuredly very hungry.

13

Before Chicago became a city, law enforcement was informal with protection provided by soldiers at Fort Dearborn. In 1831, there were 350 settlers in Chicago. They voted for incorporation and elected their first Board of Trustees. The trustees had a log jailhouse built. There were, however, no provisions for law enforcement officers to be hired or appointed.

The town became a city in 1837. A high constable was elected and the common council appointed one constable from each of the city's six wards. By 1855 the police force had grown to nine men.

Dr. Levi Boone, a candidate of the American Party, often called the Know-Nothing Party, was elected Chicago's mayor in 1855 and with the city council established a police department with ninety men.

The first questioning of someone arrested for murder in the city took place at the end of 1855. It is said the suspect's name was Homer William Croft, a paddleboat stoker who had steadfastly refused to admit that he had beaten a dock-worker to death with a block of wood. There had been no witnesses. But there were no rules for questioning a suspect. Croft was strong, stupid, and determined. He held out for almost two hours and emerged, according to the journal of one Simon Walsh, a clerk, with "his right eye purple swelled and looking like it was to burst and his shoulder held at a curious angle broke for certain. The man walked slow and pitiful and none would envy him his plight."

Since the questioning and confession of Homer William Croft, there had been more than a million suspects questioned. Gradually the methods had changed. Detectives had gone from beating out confessions to cajoling, coaxing, and tricking.

Hanrahan's rule number one was offer the suspect a cigarette. He kept a pack in his pocket though he had never smoked.

Paul Berg was seated in the room, which used to be called the interrogation room but now was the room with no name on the second floor about twenty steps down from the squad room.

It wasn't dawn yet and Bill's mind wasn't fully focused on the frightened-looking creature seated across the room with Sean O'Neil across from him. All they needed was a chess- or checkerboard between them. Bill had somewhere else he wanted to get to, get to as quickly as he could, which meant that he would make a special effort to be careful in this interrogation, not to hurry, not to make a mistake.

He sat next to O'Neil across from Berg. The tape recorder lay on the table between them.

"We're taping," said Hanrahan. "Okay?"

Berg rubbed his mouth, folded his hands on the table in front of him, looked at the tape recorder, and shrugged.

Bill pulled the package of Winstons from his pocket, held them out to Berg, who took them and removed one cigarette, which Hanrahan lit.

"I'm going to turn it on now," said Hanrahan, "and ask you again. This time answer the question."

Hanrahan reached over and pressed the button on the machine.

HANRAHAN: We're taping this conversation with Paul Berg on Wednesday morning, six-twelve, May third. Mr. Berg?

BERG: Yeah, okay.

HANRAHAN: Your name is Paul Seymour Berg. You are twenty years old. Right?

BERG: Yeah, right.

O'NEIL: Did you shoot—

HANRAHAN: Do you want a lawyer?

BERG: No, not now. I want to talk.

O'NEIL: Did you shoot Daniel Rostinski and George Grosse in the living room of the house you live in yesterday?

BERG: Yes.

HANRAHAN: Why?

BERG: We had an argument. A fight.

O'NEIL: About what?

BERG: I don't know. What music we should put on the CD, something. I got mad. We fought.

HANRAHAN: They hit you? You hit them?

BERG: Yeah.

HANRAHAN: There were no marks on their knuckles and no bruises on their bodies. There are no marks on you or your knuckles.

BERG: Whatever. Maybe we didn't hit each other. We get . . . got mad at each other a lot.

HANRAHAN: They were both sitting.

BERG: I guess.

HANRAHAN: So you were just arguing and decided to shoot them where they sat?

BERG: I lost my temper. I lose my temper a lot. Always did.

O'NEIL: Why didn't you throw the gun away?

BERG: I don't know. Thought maybe I'd shoot myself or go down shooting it with you guys.

HANRAHAN: How many shots did you fire?

BERG: Don't remember.

O'NEIL: Neighbor across the street says three shots. One in each of your buddies and a third one about ten seconds later.

HANRAHAN: We found the third bullet in the wall. Why did you fire a third time? Why did you wait ten seconds? Why did you miss by fifteen feet?

BERG: I don't know. I don't remember. I don't know.

O'NEIL: We've got you for six assaults, three counts of rape, and the murder of an old woman.

BERG: I'm not talking about any of that. For that I want a lawyer.

HANRAHAN: You didn't use a gun in any of those assaults or the murder of the old woman. Where did you get the gun?

BERG: From the shop.

O'NEIL: Your father's burger place?

BERG: Yeah, he keeps it there by the register. We've been robbed three times.

HANRAHAN: How long have you had the gun? Your father says it was by the register when he came in yesterday morning.

BERG: I got it in the morning. Early.

HANRAHAN: Why?

O'NEIL: You already planned to kill your buddies.

BERG: Maybe.

HANRAHAN: So you had an argument with your friends, pulled out the gun when your grandmother walked in . . .

BERG: She walked in after I shot them.

HANRAHAN: Your grandmother walks in, starts screaming, and you run. That the way it happened?

BERG: That's the way.

O'NEIL: Your father and grandmother want to talk to you.

BERG: I don't want to talk to them. I don't want to see them. I don't have to, right?

HANRAHAN: No, but . . .

BERG: Now I want a lawyer.

Hanrahan reached over and pushed a button. The tape recorder stopped humming, and O'Neil asked, "You know a cop named Morton?"

"Detective O'Neil, the man asked for a lawyer," Bill said.

"Black cop?" said O'Neil.

"No," said Berg, looking puzzled.

"Sean," Hanrahan warned.

"Never saw him yesterday?" asked O'Neil.

"I don't know any cop named Morton," Berg said. "I confessed. You got the fuckin' tape. I'm not talking anymore."

"Just sit here," Bill said to Berg. "You want a cup of coffee, something?"

"Coke," Berg said, running fingers through his hair, his head bent.

The two detectives left the room, closed the door, and stood facing Captain Kearney, whose eyes were on Berg through the one-way mirror. An assistant state's attorney named Sandra Whitney stood next to him, her lips pursed in thought. She was short, thin, athletic-looking, and not very happy.

"Full of holes," she said.

Kearney nodded.

"He planned the whole thing," said O'Neil. "Maybe to keep them quiet about the rapes, the murder of the old woman."

"Took the gun from the shop, went with them to his own home, shot them in the living room where people could hear it. What was the plan? How was he going to get the bodies out?" asked Whitney.

O'Neil shrugged.

"Probably planned to claim it was a home invasion," said O'Neil.

"No, Detective," she said. "He's probably going to be told by a lawyer that you coerced the confession because you were trying to cover for a fellow officer."

"A . . . ," O'Neil began.

"Hugh Morton. You suggested it to him. In addition to which, he can read, watch television. And he'll have a lawyer who certainly does. Berg raped Morton's wife. And you practically handed him an out."

"No, wait . . . ," O'Neil began.

"Gun from his father's shop," said Kearney. "Confession."

"The business about waiting ten seconds to shoot the third time opens doors I don't want opened," she said.

"Maybe he's going for insanity," said O'Neil. "He's got the murder of the old lady, the attacks, rapes."

"Maybe," said Kearney. "But he kept the damn gun. Why?"

"He's stupid," said O'Neil.

"No, he's not," said Hanrahan.

"Then what the hell is he?" said O'Neil.

"Maybe innocent," said Hanrahan.

The *alter cockers*, not yet finished with their first coffee and bagel with a schmear and a few slices of Nova or smoked whitefish, were evenly divided on the issue of the morning.

Their voices were raised when Abe walked in and while a few of them noted his coming they were too deeply into the debate to pause.

Lieberman made his way to his booth. The counter wasn't full but there were customers. Rose Shlovsky was reading the *Sun-Times*, adjusting her glasses. She lived right around the corner. She worked downtown on Michigan Avenue. She would drive to the El and take it to work when she finished. She had done the same thing five days a week for the past six years except for the two weeks each year when she went on a cruise and the time she had Asian flu. She looked over her newspaper and nodded at Abe. Then she looked over her shoulder at the *alter cockers* and let out her long-suffering sigh as Herschel Rosen raised his voice.

A cab driver named Latif something sat next to Rose Shlovsky. Lieberman couldn't remember his last name at the moment, something without vowels; he was talking to Maish, who leaned toward him and nodded.

A couple sat at one of the booths. A trio of Devon Avenue salesmen sat at another, talking quietly.

Over his shoulder through the opening to the kitchen Lieberman could see Terrell, the cook. Terrell was dropping a couple of bagels in the toaster. Their eyes met. Terrell wiped his brow with his sleeve and nodded. Their conspiracy was under way.

"The master detective is back," said Bloomberg at the *alter cockers*' table. "Maybe this mystery he can unravel."

"What mystery?" Rosen said with disdain. "The woman's pregnant. Her husband claims he's impotent."

"Sterile," Howie Chen corrected.

"Whatever," said Rosen with a sigh of exasperation. "Says

he knew it for more than a year. Doctor told him when he went in for a routine prostate. Didn't tell his wife. Kept *shtuping* . . ."

"Rosen," Bloomberg said. "People are listening. A lady is listening."

"Rose has heard it all," said Rosen. "Right, Rosie?"

Rose didn't answer.

"Who're you talking about?" asked Maish.

"Larry Zolner, Larry and Evie," said Rosen.

"Evie's pregnant?" asked Maish.

The salesmen in the booth stopped talking. Larry Zolner owned the hardware store two blocks down a few doors off of California. They all knew him.

"Larry Zolner's sterile?" asked one of the salesmen.

"I got to repeat everything," Rosen said. "Sterile. Yes."

"And he had a prostate problem?" asked another of the salesmen.

"Didn't I just say," said Rosen.

"How do you know all this?" said the first salesman.

"Gentlemen," he said with a sigh, looking at the other *alter cockers*. They all nodded to confirm Rosen's tale.

"She says it was him," said Bloomberg. "Couldn't be anyone else. She says she is a faithful wife."

"Spontaneous regeneration," said Chen.

"Immaculate conception," said Abe.

"Someone's lying," said Bloomberg.

"I can take them both down to the station and beat the truth out of them," Abe suggested as Maish brought him a cup of coffee.

"That would work," said Bloomberg.

"I wash my hands of you all," said Rosen, raising his

hands. "Where's the Irish? He knows about immaculate conception."

"Late," said Lieberman. "Busy."

Terrell put a plate on the counter behind Maish, who turned, picked it up, looked at it, looked at Terrell, shook his head, and carried the plate to his brother.

"Corned beef and sausage omelet?" Maish said.

"Celebration of my return," said Abe, reaching for the ketchup.

"Your arteries wait in gleeful anticipation," said Maish. "I promised Bess."

"Exceptions are necessary if rules are to have meaning," said Abe, reaching for the salt.

Maish took the salt from him before he could pour it.

"What's your cholesterol, Abraham?"

"Within the bounds of reason," Abe said, cutting into the omelet. "What's yours?"

"*Ich veis,*" said Maish. "Who knows? I'm not the one with the worried wife."

"Yetta is worried," Lieberman corrected. "But not about your cholesterol."

"Yeah," said Maish, looking at a Korean travel agent named Roland Park who worked across the street. Park was in a hurry. He was always in a hurry. Park always looked worried. He was quite willing to tell you why. The travel agency business was going the way of the rabbit ear antenna and the Cabbage Patch doll. The Internet had forced Roland Park back to school to work on computer programming. He had no place to go, but he was in a hurry.

Park sat at the counter and looked at Maish, who moved to take his order.

The *alter cockers* argued. Abe ate and drank his coffee. He checked his watch, and then punched in a number on his cell phone as Bloomberg raised his voice to say, "I have to listen to such nonsense?"

Bill knocked at the door of the apartment on Spaulding fifteen minutes from the T&L deli where he was supposed to meet Abe.

No answer. He knocked louder. There was a button for a buzzer. Bill Hanrahan saw it and decided not to use it. He pounded on the door.

The door opened. In front of him, wearing a blue linen robe with a darker blue sash, stood Jon Li, lean, late twenties, clean-shaven, smiling.

"Come in," he said, stepping out of the way.

"You know who I am," Hanrahan said. It wasn't a question.

"Yes," said Li. "I have been expecting you."

The room into which he was ushered was big, light with early-morning sun and sparsely but neatly furnished with minimalist monotone chairs made of something that looked to Hanrahan like linen. There was no sofa, no television. On the wall was a single photo about the size of a newspaper page. The photo was of a Chinese man about fifty with a knowing smile.

"That is Li Hongzhi," Jon Li said, seeing Hanrahan's glance at the photograph. "Please sit."

"No thanks."

Li nodded and stood facing his guest, hands folded in front of him. Bill was about half a foot taller than Li. The detective felt the tiny throbbing in his forehead that meant either a headache or the loss of control. In the past, before he had gone sober, he had quelled its demands with scotch. Now he relied on self-control, which occasionally worked.

"You don't call me again. You don't call my wife again," Hanrahan said, taking a step forward to invade Li's space.

Li did not back away.

"She is my cousin," Li said.

"She is my wife," said Hanrahan.

"Do you know anything about Falun Gong, Falun Dafa?"

"A Chinese cult," said Hanrahan. "Iris told me. Banned by the Chinese government."

"Not a cult," said Li with a tolerant nod of his head. "Not a religion. A certain knowledge discovered by Li Hongzhi not ten years ago. Master Hongzhi now lives in the United States, in New York. I have seen him."

"I don't give a shit," said Hanrahan, feeling the tension in his palms, the tightening of his fists.

"The Great Law of the Dharma Wheel," said Li in the same monotone in which he had been speaking. "The wheel is a miniature of the cosmos that Master Hongzhi can install telekinetically in the abdomen of those who follow him. The wheel rotates in alternating directions."

Li moved his right hand slowly in a circle in front of his stomach in one direction and then reversed the movement.

"The wheel throws off bad karma. We can feel the wheel turning in our bellies."

"I told you, I don't—"

Li held up his right hand, palm out about six inches from Hanrahan's face.

"You do," said Li. "Master Hongzhi tells us that humanity will soon be erased by aliens from space. To take one's place in heaven, one must accept certain truths."

"I know it won't do any good," said Hanrahan, "but I'm going to say it anyway. You are a goddamn lunatic."

Hanrahan's cell phone played the first seven notes of "Danny Boy." He considered ignoring it, but didn't.

"Hanrahan," he said, eyes on Li.

"Father Murph, where are you? You all right?"

"Fine, Rabbi. Be there in a little while."

"The *alter cockers* have a question of theology they want you to settle," said Lieberman.

"When I finish with what I'm doing," he said, "I'll be happy to take care of it."

"You're in a hurry?" said Abe.

"I am, Rabbi," said Bill. "See you soon."

He hung up.

"You are not Jewish," said Li.

"I am not."

"Yet you talk intimately with a rabbi."

"I'm open-minded."

"No, you are not. Would you like me to tell you why I called Iris and you?" Li said, unperturbed.

"Tell it fast," said Hanrahan.

There was a distinct, demanding throbbing in his forehead now.

"In Master Hongzhi's view, the races are not to be intermingled. Mixed-race children are symptoms of society's decline. Each race has its own particular 'biosphere,' and whenever children are born of a mixed-race relationship, they are 'defective persons.' Heaven itself is segregated. Anyone who does not belong to his own race will not be cared for."

"You are definitely nuts."

"No, it is true. I am revealing the secret of heaven to you as it was revealed to me," said Li. "You are a Catholic?"

"Yeah."

"And you believe a man named Jesus was created by your single God and by believing in him, simply believing, you will go to heaven?"

"Something like that," said Hanrahan.

"Miracles, saints, walking on water?" said Li. "And an old man in Italy is spoken to by your Jesus and tells you what to do, how to behave, what to think? And I am mad?"

"I'm not here to talk about religion," said Hanrahan. "I'm here to tell you that if you call again, either one of us, I'm going to throw you out a window."

Li closed his eyes and then opened them.

"Then as the wheel turns inside me, I shall levitate as Master Hongzhi says that I can."

"Levitate? Float?"

"Your saints levitated. The Master has seen your own David Copperfield levitate."

"I'll kill you if you threaten my wife, my child."

"Warn, not threaten," Li corrected. "Have you ever killed?"

"Yes," said Hanrahan.

Li looked into the detective's eyes, waited a beat, and said, "Yes, you have."

"No more calls," said Hanrahan. "Stay away from us."

"I am trying to save you," said Li. "Are you not ordered by your church to try to save those who do not believe by converting them to your truth?"

"I'm not a priest," said Hanrahan.

"And I am not a priest," said Li. "But I wish to save my cousin and stop the birth of a—"

Hanrahan reached out, grabbed the lapels of Li's robe, and pushed. Li fell backward, foot up into Hanrahan's stomach. Hanrahan tumbled to the floor onto his left shoulder. When he looked up, Li was standing, smiling.

"Master Hongzhi teaches very ancient martial arts," he said.

Hanrahan got to one knee, his bad knee. It hurt, but not enough to keep him from standing. He had a strong desire to pull out his weapon and shoot the smiling, self-satisfied man in front of him. Instead, he leaned over to rub his sore knee as Li said,

"If you—"

But he didn't finish. Hanrahan shot his head upward into the chin of the smaller man. He heard a cracking sound. The shock flashed through Bill's head. He looked up. Li had staggered back, blood dripping from his mouth.

"Take a step toward me and I shoot your sorry ass," Bill said.

Li's eyes were watering. His mouth opened to speak, but the pain was too great.

"I think your jaw's broken," said Hanrahan. "Turn the wheel and make it better and when it's healed, don't call us."

He took a step toward the door, turned to look at Li again, and repeated emphatically, "Do not call us."

Bill closed the door gently behind him. He was reasonably certain that he had not heard the last of the fanatic. He would try to talk to Iris's father, but he didn't think that would work. He had seen too many followers of cults and mad leaders to think that anyone could change the mind of a true believer.

He went down the stairs thinking that there might well come a time soon when he would have to kill Jon Li.

Sean O'Neil got to the Clean Cut barbershop just as Monty was picking up the newspaper in front of the door.

"Detective O'Neil," Monty said, tucking the newspaper under his arm and opening the door with one of about thirty keys on his chain. "Early bird. We've got no early bird special."

Monty chuckled at his joke as he turned on the fluorescent lights. He looked at O'Neil, who was taking off his jacket. His holster was clipped to his belt. Sean O'Neil was not smiling at the barber's wit.

Monty took off his sweater and brushed off his barber chair. The lights above pinged slowly to life.

O'Neil sat in the chair.

"Looking a little P and O'd this A.M.," said Monty.

"Having a bad morning," said O'Neil. "Cut it like always."

"Like always," said Monty.

"So, any inside stuff you can tell me about the world of crime so I can have material for the day?"

"Don't feel much like talking this morning," said O'Neil.

"I'll talk," said Monty, starting to work on O'Neil's hair. "You know Wayne Czerbiak?"

O'Neil grunted, thinking about the interrogation of Berg and Hanrahan's upstaging him.

"I told you about him yesterday, on the phone. Or was it the day before."

O'Neil didn't bother to grunt.

"Says he has a gun," said Monty, combing and cutting. "Says he's going to shoot someone today."

"The sign painter? The one with the goofy smile?" asked O'Neil without really paying attention.

"How many Wayne Czerbiaks you think there are in Chicago?" asked Monty. "I mean, who come in here?"

Monty smiled. He was at his best and it wasn't even nine in the morning yet.

"I think he has a gun," said Monty. "His father, you remember his father? Nice man. Strict. Old World, but a nice man. No sense of humor, though. Wayne's too far the other way. Smiles at everything. Never know if he thinks what you're saying is funny. Know what I mean?"

"I know," said O'Neil.

"Goofy kind of guy," said Monty. "Might be he means it."

"Okay," said O'Neil. "Where does the dumb Polack live?"

"He's not Polish," said Monty. "Hungarian or Czech or something."

"Monty, where does he live?"

"Over on Troy, a few blocks down. Sign in the window says 'Czerbiak's Signs.' Can't miss it. You going over there?"

"Just finish the haircut."

Hanrahan arrived at the T&L to the greeting of Herschel Rosen who called out, "The Irish Republican Army has arrived. We can get our answer."

"What's your question?" asked Hanrahan, sitting across from Lieberman and putting down the folded newspaper he had brought with him.

There was nothing in front of Abe but a cup of coffee. He had finished his omelet, eaten slowly, fifteen minutes earlier.

"It's about immaculate conception," said Rosen.

"It's overrated," said Hanrahan.

The *alter cockers* laughed.

"Enough," said Hurwitz, the retired psychologist who, at the age of eighty-three, was the oldest of the *alter cockers*, a position of no particular esteem but some respect that he seldom exerted.

Maish brought a cup of coffee and placed it in front of Hanrahan.

"What's the special?" asked Hanrahan.

"Three eggs any way you like, flank steak, Terrell's special fries, coffee, onion bagel, and convivial conversation and kibitzing, four dollars."

"I'll take it," said Hanrahan. "Eggs scrambled and soft."

Maish moved away and Hanrahan looked across the table at his partner.

"What?" asked Hanrahan.

"What? You look like you want me to say your shirt is blue and not white so you can shove it down my throat is what," said Lieberman.

"Sorry," said Hanrahan. "Tough morning."

"Apology accepted. Want to talk about it?"

"Maybe. Later. I've got a favor."

"To give or get?" asked Lieberman.

"Get. I'd like you to talk to a suspect," said Hanrahan. "I think you'll get further than I would."

"You underestimate yourself, Father Murph."

"No, I know my suspect, Rabbi. And we're running out of time if we're going to keep a cop from getting crucified."

He unfolded the newspaper, placed it in front of Lieberman, and pointed to a story at the bottom of the front page.

"You know Hugh Morton?" asked Hanrahan.

"Slightly," said Lieberman. "Good man. I met his wife once, too."

"We've got one of guys who raped her and broke her arm," said Hanrahan. "Says he killed his two partners. Confession stinks. Morton stays on the front page and the suspect list at least until we lock it down."

"And?"

"If we don't lock it down fast, Morton's going to be on the evening news with hints that he killed the two rapists.

The public will be on his side. The mayor won't be able to erase the publicity."

"Tell me about it," Abe said and while they waited for the steak-and-egg special and while Bill ate it and while the *alter cockers* argued, cackled, predicted, and prodded, Hanrahan told the story.

O'Neil walked up the six concrete steps of the small brick house with the sign in the window. He knocked. No answer. He knocked again and tried the door. It wasn't locked.

He opened the door about six inches and called Wayne's name.

No answer.

What the hell. He went in. The place was clean, neat, but it didn't look like a home. The area where there should have been a living room was an open workspace with a huge table covered with piles of board and rows of paint, pens, pencils, rulers, and books. All neat. All orderly.

"Wayne, you here?" he called, moving through the workroom toward a room in front of him. He pushed open the door. A kitchen. Spotless.

O'Neil moved to his left to another door. The door was closed. He knocked. No answer. He opened the door and stepped in.

There was a single bed, neatly made. A dresser, its top flat, clear, polished. A table with a black-and-white television on it a few feet from the bed and an old armchair in the corner.

Sean O'Neil saw none of this. What he saw was a huge full-color photograph of a young man in jeans, a T-shirt, and a cowboy hat. The young man was playing a guitar. His mouth was open and if it weren't for the guitar, you could swear he was being tortured.

In neat white letters across the top of the poster were the words *Commemorating the short brightly burning life of Lee Cole Carter. Died at the hands of his admirer Wayne Czerbiak on this date of* . . ."

There were two dates. One was neatly x-ed out in blue. Next to it in fresh white was today's date.

14

Parker Liao was on a mission. It had an upside and a down-side.

The downside was that he was doing it as a favor for Mr. Woo, which meant it was an order. The reason Parker owed Mr. Woo a favor was that Mr. Woo had, with the help of the Jewish policeman named Lieberman, prevented a gang killing that would have resulted in the embarrassment of Liao and the Twin Dragons, not to mention the possibility that young Chinese men would most surely have died in an exchange of fire with the Puerto Ricans.

The upside of Liao's mission was that it gave him the opportunity to do what he did best.

There were two members of the Twin Dragons with him, one on either side, both dressed in black suits, black T-shirts. Parker Liao wore the same.

He knocked at the apartment door.

Jon Li opened it. He was now wearing tan slacks and a white short-sleeved shirt with button-down collar and no tie.

Their eyes met. Li smiled. Parker Liao did not.

Parker Liao and Jon Li were approximately the same age and height. The two men behind Liao were younger, just a bit shorter.

"You know who I am?" said Liao.

"I know."

"You know why I am here?"

"I know."

"And you will make no more calls, have no more contact with Mrs. Hanrahan."

"Miss Chen," Li amended.

"Mrs. Hanrahan," Liao repeated.

They were still standing in the doorway of the apartment.

"I will do what I must for the spiritual deliverance of my cousin," said Li.

"There is no more to say," said Liao. "If you contact her in any way, you die."

Li smiled and stepped back to let them in.

"We don't wish your hospitality," said Liao.

"I thought it might be more private and personal if your people were to beat me in my home rather than the hall."

"You are Falun Gong," said Liao.

Li closed his eyes and bowed his head and then looked up again.

"You are therefore a madman," Liao said. "Beating would almost certainly please you."

"You could break my legs," said Li. "Or my hands? No, better, you could cut out my tongue."

"Thank you for the helpful suggestions," said Liao. "But I prefer things be kept simple. You stop or you die."

"Mr. Woo sent you."

Parker stood, hands folded in front of him, and said nothing.

"Mr. Woo is the self-appointed protector of my cousin Iris Chen. He is a thief, a murderer, a dealer in crimes against the chosen people."

"The Jews?" asked Parker.

"The Chinese," said Li. "And even with his crimes it would have been better had he married my cousin and that she have his baby. But then, Mr. Woo is a very old man."

"He is," said Parker. "And I think it likely you will never be."

Li shrugged.

"I am to stop trying to convince my cousin to have this unclean child aborted or I shall die. Correct?"

"Yes."

"Then there is nothing more to be said," Li said, reaching to close the door.

Parker held his left hand out and placed it on the door to keep Li from shutting it. The Twin Dragon on Parker's left stepped into the apartment past Li, careful not to touch him.

The man strode to the wall, took down the photograph of Hongzhi, and brought it to Parker. Li watched. He seemed curious and amused.

Parker turned the frame around, removed the photograph, slowly tore it in half, and handed it to Li.

"It's just paper," Li said. "I shall get another one."

The three Twin Dragons left and Li closed the door.

Parker Liao said nothing. He had failed to intimidate the madman. Parker regarded all religion as distasteful. It was one of the very few things he shared with the Communists in China.

Parker had no doubt that Li would call Iris Chen again. He had no doubt that he would have to kill the smiling little bastard. There would be no satisfaction in doing it or having it done. For death to be meaningful, one must care about his life.

"He's upstairs now," said Richie the doorman. "Just missed him. He won't stay long, never does."

"I'll wait," said Wayne.

"Gonna shoot him today," said Richie.

"Gonna shoot him today," Wayne repeated.

"Little camera?"

"Yes," said Wayne.

Richie had been three years ahead of Wayne at Lakeview High. They hadn't been friends. They hadn't been enemies. All they shared was the fact that neither participated in anything at school. Not football, baseball, basketball, wrestling, the photo club, the collectors club, the herpetology club, the Young Republicans, nothing.

Wayne had painted all the signs for school dances, elections, meetings, none of which he attended. Everything he had created had been thrown away or washed away by the wind, rain, and time. All these years since he barely graduated, Wayne had continued to do the signs for homecomings, graduation, the Methodist church rummage sale, the community flower festival.

Reasons, Wayne thought as he waited for the elevator, reasons he could have given had he been asked about what he planned to do in a few minutes:

Lee Cole Carter had been against the war with Iraq. He was unpatriotic.

Lee Cole Carter had done nothing for the very neighborhood in which he was born.

Lee Cole Carter took the Lord's name in vain in his songs.

Lee Cole Carter fornicated.

Lee Cole Carter was planning something big and evil. Wayne wasn't sure what it was, but it was clearly spelled out in his songs. Well, maybe not so clearly, but it was there.

Lee Cole Carter had one of those smug I'm-a-star faces that let you know he thought you were a dust mite and he knew something funny and embarrassing about you.

Lee Cole Carter's death would make Wayne famous for a little while. He'd be interviewed by Diane Sawyer just before the weather on *Good Morning America*.

Lee Cole Carter's death would put Wayne in prison forever and he'd never have to make another decision again about much of anything. Maybe they'd let him paint signs till the arthritis got him the way it had gotten his father. Did they need someone to paint signs in prison?

These were all reasons he might give. One or two of them might even be right, or maybe not.

"Carters expecting you, Wayne?" asked Richie.

"No."

"Gotta call them up then," he said with a deep sigh as if the sigh were a major task.

The elevator doors opened when Richie was dialing. Out stepped Lee Cole Carter. He was wearing a cowboy hat, nice tan one with a black band and a tiny feather. His face was shaved clean, a concession to his parents, because when he did his videos or TV appearances Lee Cole always looked like he needed a shave.

He was also wearing clean new-looking jeans and a Dallas Cowboys shirt, not the T-kind but a white one with a collar and just a little Dallas Cowboys insignia on the pocket.

He was smoking, looked deep in thought, didn't see Richie or Wayne. He walked past them toward the door.

"Mr. Carter," Richie called.

Lee Cole paused and turned, his mind still somewhere,

maybe upstairs with his parents, maybe in some studio in
Nashville or in bed with some girl. He looked at Richie.

"Wayne wants to shoot you," Richie said. "That all right?"

Lee Cole Carter looked at Wayne, head to foot, maybe
recognizing something.

"Shoot me?"

"Picture, photograph, you know," Richie explained.

Wayne's hand was in his pocket. The gun felt surprisingly
warm. He imagined, tasted gun metal in his mouth, on his
tongue.

"Wayne Czerbiak?" asked Lee Cole, taking a step toward
Wayne.

Wayne nodded.

"You painted the horse on the sidewalk in front of Lakeview High for the homecoming when I graduated."

"Yeah," said Wayne.

Lee Cole smiled.

"Great horse. Forgot about that till just now. Funny how
you forget things and they just come back."

"I've got a poem about a horse," Richie lied. "I can get it
to you at the hotel before you leave."

Lee Cole wasn't listening.

"You still painting?" Lee Cole asked, taking a deep drag
on his cigarette.

"Signs," said Wayne.

"That horse," Lee Cole said, looking up at the ceiling,
maybe trying to see the horse. "All white and wide-eyed. It
had wings or a horn on its head or something."

"Both," said Wayne. "A flying unicorn."

"Flying unicorn," Lee Cole repeated almost to himself.

"Well, I'll be damned," Richie lied again. "My poem is
about a white flying unicorn."

"It'd make a good album cover," Lee Cole said, looking at

Wayne. "I could write a song about homecoming, that horse, Connie Appleton, but I wouldn't use her name. You know."

Richie sighed. He wasn't getting through. He knew it. He was doomed by his uniform.

"You got a card?" Lee Cole asked.

"No," said Wayne.

"Well, you can write your name and number down for me and I'll have someone call you."

"You'd forget," said Wayne. "You'd shove it in your pocket and forget and five months from now you'd forget why you wrote my name and number and throw it away."

Lee Cole adjusted his cowboy hat and grinned.

"You may be right, but don't count on it. You want to take my picture?"

"No," said Wayne, taking the gun out of his pocket and aiming it at the singer.

There were several ways to go about this. Lieberman could have done it at the station in the interrogation room or he could have borrowed Captain Kearney's office. He could have done it at the Berg house. Scene of the crime. He could have done it at Berg's Burgers. All had drawbacks. He wasn't going for intimidation and he didn't want to create an atmosphere of fear or horror. He wanted intimacy.

He settled on a small park where they could sit under the roof of a pavilion. It was still early. There were only a few people in the park, young mothers with their babies talking at a bench, a trio of old men, two of whom had canes, one of whom had a walker.

The wooden table of the pavilion had been painted recently to cover the rough graffiti, crudely carved hearts, tic-

tac-toe games played with knives. The painting was a regular
event to try to keep the parks looking like parks and not the
first day of the end of days.

Abe and Bill sat on one side of the bench, Paul Berg and
his grandmother across from them. A tape recorder lay on
the table between them.

The woman, who was probably only a few years older
than Lieberman, was pale; her hair needed combing. She
hugged herself as if she were cold, but it wasn't cold. Her
grandson, wearing a gray sweatshirt with little black letters
reading *Bay Yacht Club* folded his hands on the table.

"Meeting here okay with you?" asked Lieberman.

"I don't know," Paul Berg said, looking around uncom-
fortably. "You asked us to come here."

"We can go to the station," Abe said.

"No, here is fine."

Lieberman pushed the *on* button.

"I'm Detective Abraham Lieberman. My partner is . . ."

"Detective William Hanrahan," Bill supplied.

"And," Lieberman continued, "we're talking to Bert Berg
and his mother Trudy Berg."

Lieberman stated the date and time and said, "Paul has
confessed to the murder of his friends."

"We know," said Bert, looking away.

Trudy Berg nodded her head.

"Paul's done some very bad things," said Lieberman. "You
know what they are."

"We know what the police told us they are," said Trudy.
"He didn't do those things. I don't mean he's innocent. He
was there, but it was the other two, the crazy, stupid . . .
they did those things. Those other two. Paul went along,
drove the car. He was afraid. That's no excuse, but . . ."

"He was the leader, wasn't he," said Abe.

"Leader?" said Trudy. "If you mean he was smarter than they were, yes, but they were dangerous."

"So he decided yesterday to kill them?" asked Lieberman.

"They probably threatened to kill Paul if he stopped," Trudy said, urging the detectives to understand, to believe.

"So he just picked yesterday, invited them over, brought the gun from your store, and killed them," Lieberman said.

"Ask him," said Trudy. "They had raped that poor woman in front of her kid. Broke her arm. That poor policeman. He . . . Yes, Pauly had enough. He took the gun from the shop, went home, and shot them."

"No," said Lieberman.

"No?" asked Trudy, looking at Hanrahan.

"No," Lieberman repeated. "Too many holes in the tale. My partner asked himself why a person like Paul would confess to a crime he didn't commit, a double murder. And why he would refuse to confess to a handful of muggings, rapes, and a murder he did commit. My partner couldn't think it was for anything honorable because, let us face it, Paul is not a decent or honorable young man."

"He is," Trudy Berg said emphatically, looking at Lieberman.

"Well," said Lieberman. "Maybe he is for once. Here's the way my partner sees it. Mrs. Berg, you got up in the morning and read in the papers or saw the story of the policeman's wife being attacked. You knew Paul and his friends were at your house. You took the gun, went home, walked into your living room, and shot them."

"You're . . . ," Berg began, and started to rise.

His mother put her hand on his. He looked at her, a question in his eyes, and sat again.

"Were you going to shoot your grandson, too?" asked Lieberman.

"We want a lawyer," said Bert Berg, starting to rise again.

"You can have one," said Lieberman. "You don't have to say a word. Just listen. Can you do that? Will you do that?"

"We don't say a word without a lawyer."

"Understood," said Lieberman.

There was a long pause and Lieberman continued, "You were standing there with a gun in your hand. Your grandson took it from you and fired it into the wall."

"Why would . . . ?" Bert began, and then remembered his vow of silence.

"Residue," said Lieberman. "When we caught him, and he knew we would, he wanted the evidence to show that he had fired the gun. He wanted to have that gun when he was found. Your grandson was protecting you, Mrs. Berg. He's still trying to protect you."

She opened her mouth to speak but her son said, "Ma," and she closed her mouth again, though her lower lip was now quivering.

"Did he say anything to you, Mrs. Berg? Did your grandson say anything to you?"

"He . . ."

"Ma," Bert warned.

She shrugged him off and said, "Pauly said that he was going to go to jail for the things he had been doing. He said things wouldn't be worse for his being the one who shot his friends. The police didn't care about his two friends."

"Ma," Bert said, but it was no longer a warning. It was a deep sigh of defeat.

"He said," she went on, "that he didn't want me to go to jail or have a trial. He made me promise to say he had shot them, but then this policeman . . ." She looked at Hanrahan. "And the other big one came through the front door and Pauly, he ran and I said I hadn't seen the shooting."

Berg reached over and turned off the tape recorder.

"We should have had a lawyer," he said. "I watch *Law and Order*. You'll never be allowed to use this tape and my mother isn't going to speak about this."

"Then your son goes to jail for the rest of his life," said Lieberman.

"Maybe that's where he should be. Maybe it's my fault."

"There's plenty of guilt to go around," said Lieberman.

"Let's go," said Bert, now taking his mother's arm.

She removed his hand from her arm, looked at Lieberman, and said, "You have grandchildren?"

"Two."

"Are they good kids?"

"Yes," said Lieberman.

"Our Pauly was bar mitzvahed," she said. "Did you know that?"

"No," said Lieberman. "My grandson Barry has his bar mitzvah this weekend."

"I hope he takes his vows seriously," said Trudy. "I knew when Pauly had his bar mitzvah he was just saying words."

There was nothing to say. Lieberman, still sitting next to Hanrahan, nodded.

"I'll say it all again, about the shooting," she said. "Whenever you like if you need it. Pauly's done his good deed. But it's too late."

"Can we go now?" asked Berg. His eyes were moist now.

He took his mother's hand, looked at the ground and then up at Lieberman.

"Are you going to arrest me?" she asked.

"Your grandson confessed," Lieberman said. "That's enough

to convict him. Getting him on the other murder, the murder of a woman about your age, will be a lot harder, and rape trials are always tough on the victims. And, as you said, it'll be hard to get this tape admitted into evidence."

"So . . . ?" Bert began.

"We'll let you know," said Lieberman.

The detectives stayed at the bench watching mother and son, hand in hand, walk slowly down the path through the grass, past the old men on one bench and the young mothers and their small children at the other.

"Thanks, Rabbi," said Hanrahan.

It was unspoken. It needed no words. Bill had asked his partner to conduct the meeting because he was Jewish like Trudy, because he looked and sounded like the kind of person you want to confess to. Bill was not that kind of person.

"You're welcome, Father Murph," he said. "What do we do with it? It's your call."

"We've got a confession," said Hanrahan.

"That we have," Lieberman agreed as they walked.

"From a rapist and murderer," Hanrahan said.

"No more need be said," said Lieberman, removing the tape from the recorder and handing it to his partner.

"Now there's one you can do for me," said Lieberman.

Emiliano "El Perro" Del Sol was wearing a suit and tie. The suit had been a gift from Gerardo Econecho Lopez, who had a clothing store one block from El Perro's bingo parlor headquarters next door to El Perro's restaurant.

People in the neighborhood gave El Perro gifts. Some of the gifts were given to ward off the Tentaculo leader's bursts of madness. Some of the gifts were given out of a real sense of gratitude. While the Tentaculos might prey on the Latino community in their territory, they did not bleed the shop and business owners. Well, not much. And the other gangs and the shaky kids looking for drug money or something they could sell stayed out of Tentaculo territory.

And so Emiliano Del Sol, king of North Avenue, had dressed in a suit and tie and ordered three of his men to do the same. Even Piedras was wearing a suit and tie.

"We look fuckin' *guapo*," said El Perro. "You called Taibo?"

Juan Hernandez said, "*Sí*. He'll be there."

"*Bueno*," said El Perro, admiring himself in the mirror of the men's room of the bingo parlor. "Let's go show them chinks some cool."

"Wayne," Richie cried out from behind the desk.

Lee Cole Carter looked at the gun and lost his grin.

"Hold it, Wayne. I've got about five hundred dollars in the wallet. I'll just pull it out and hand it over. Put the gun away and we'll call it a loan, no, a first payment for the flying-horse album cover."

"Not about money," said Wayne. "I've got eleven thousand four hundred and six dollars in savings at the Bank of America."

"I do something to you?" asked Lee Cole. "I mean you got a grudge, something? I knock up your sister or cousin or something, insult you or your family? Hell, I was a kid."

"You're everybody," Wayne said as Lee Cole started to raise his arms, though no one had asked him to.

Lee Cole glanced at Richie for help. Richie had none.

The idea had just come to Wayne. Right out of the blue, nowhere. Lee Cole Carter was everybody. Lee Cole Carter wasn't just a country singer who used to live in Bardo, Texas. Lee Cole was Texas, was the United States, was the world. The world had no meaning. That's what had started Wayne down this gun-weighted road. It was all made up. All a story people told each other to make them forget they were going to die and the world was going to blow up or blow away or freeze or burn someday.

Maybe Monty had said something like this once and the idea had just slept all curled up inside him and woke up just now wondering what was going on.

Wayne was going to be a shooting star. He was going to be a bright light for a few seconds. He was going to shoot a star. He was going to be a star. It was that or just keep painting signs till his fingers got too much arthritis like his father's had and then he'd live alone in the house and watch television and eat cereal with freeze-dried fruit in it that got soggy when you added milk.

Richie said, "Wayne, no."

Wayne pulled the trigger. He was no more than a dozen feet from Lee Cole Carter, but he had never fired a gun before and missed, shattering the window behind the man who had written and sung "Hard Drinking Woman."

Through the shattered window, Wayne could see a man who had frozen midstep on the sidewalk. The man was pulling out a gun. Wayne recognized the man. He was a policeman named O'Neil whom he had seen two or three times in the Clean Cut barbershop.

15

Bess answered her recently acquired cell phone after the third ring.

"Hello," she said.

"I've got to go to Yuma," said Lieberman.

"Can you talk a little louder," she said. "I'm at the temple with Lisa. We're going over . . . Did you say you've got to go to Yuma?"

"Yes," he said.

"When?"

"Tonight."

"The bar mitzvah is in two days, Abe. It can't wait?"

"I don't think so," he said.

"Where are you?"

"On the way to a meeting," he said.

"I don't like it, Abe."

"Can't be helped," he said.

She paused, considering whether to open up the question of whether or not the trip to Yuma could be helped, postponed, avoided, ignored. She considered reminding him that they had only one grandson and that if he was delayed or there was an airplane strike, or bad weather . . .

"I'll be back in time," he said.

"Will you pick Marvin up at the airport today?"

"Bill will do it."

"You've got it all worked out," she said with a sigh, looking at the sample blue-and-gold napkin Morrie Greenblatt was holding up for her final decision. She nodded her approval.

"Travel arrangements, yes," Abe said. "Approval from Kearney, yes. Airfare, no. We'll have to put it on the American Express and I'll put in for reimbursement."

"And you'll get it?"

"Probably not," he said. "But we're nearly rich, remember?"

"You have to go?" she asked with resignation.

"I have to go," he said.

"What time are you going home to pack?"

"When I can."

"I'll pack for you. The overnight will be at the door," she said.

"What would I do without you?"

"Eat badly and have a heart attack. Forget to do your laundry till the last minute. Chase after loose women."

"Two out of three," he said.

"Which two?" Bess asked as Morrie Greenblatt shuffled toward her with a sample of the table decoration for Friday night. It was hideous, blue aluminum foil around a flowerpot with a single planted plastic Israeli flag next to a white flower.

"The flower will be real," Morrie said.

"Abe, I've got to go. Don't eat Mexican food in Yuma."

"I promise."

They hung up.

Abe checked his watch and looked across the squad room for Bill. He was late and Abe had to hurry. No more time. He put on his jacket and told Ezra McDonough to tell Bill to . . . and Bill Hanrahan came through the squad room door.

"Let's go," said Lieberman.

"Sorry I'm late," said Hanrahan, who looked tired.

They went to the parking lot and got into Lieberman's car.

"You saw Paul Berg?" said Lieberman, turning south on Clark.

"Yeah," said Hanrahan. "Played him the tape. He looked like he was going to cry. He still insists he did it. How do you explain it, Rabbi? Kid rapes girls, young mothers, kills old ladies, beats people for fun, and stands up for his grandmother, willing to go down for her."

"Don't try to understand them," said Lieberman. "Just rope those cows and brand them."

"Wisdom according to *Rawhide* reruns," said Bill with a smile.

"Don't knock it," said Lieberman. "One can learn much from the Scriptures and reruns in the middle of the night. The gift of insomniacs. God keeps up awake when we want to sleep so we can glean knowledge from the secret messages sung by Frankie Laine."

"I heard he lives in San Diego, Frankie Laine," said Bill.

"You heard?"

"From Iris," Bill explained.

"Where's the tape?"

"Accidentally destroyed," said Hanrahan.

"Accidents happen, Father Murph."

"They do, Rabbi. You think this is going to work?"

"The meeting? Don't know, but it will be interesting."

Twenty minutes later they were in the small back room of the Saddle & Brew on the far Northwest side. They served Irish and English food and imported British beer. The owner was a cousin of Bill's. His name was Barney Dwyer. He was broom-handle thin, wore long-sleeve shirts year around, wore suspenders, smoked even though he had only one lung left, and supported the Irish Republican Army with rhetoric but not dollars. He also knew how to keep secrets.

Lieberman had suggested the Saddle & Brew for the meeting because it wasn't in the neighborhood of anyone coming to the table. He was sure none of the parties would be comfortable there and he was sure that since they knew the others would be uncomfortable, they would agree that Barney's place would be neutral.

It was just after one in the afternoon. Barney's wasn't crowded. Some people, mostly men, at the tables being served beer and sandwiches by Dwyer's wife Meg.

"They're here," said Dwyer, when the two detectives moved past the bar. "From the look of 'em you might have to kill the whole pack and be done with it. Meg and I will bury the bodies."

Dwyer grinned. He had good white teeth. They weren't his.

When they went through the door, they saw exactly what Abe had expected to see with one exception. A stone-faced Parker Liao sat on one side of the table with the two men who had accompanied him to Jon Li's apartment. At the far end of the table, in a conservative, brown suit, sat Mr. Woo, and a very large Chinese man in his fifties whom Bill and Abe recognized as Sidney Chao, arrested eleven times for crimes including murder, conspiracy to commit murder, assault, and a range of other colorful and violent deeds. Sidney Chao had never been convicted. He had never even been indicted.

Across from Parker Liao sat a grinning El Perro, Piedras, and a young black man in jeans and a simple blue T-shirt with a pocket over his heart. A briefcase lay on the table in front of this man.

The room smelled of years of alcohol and cigars. All eyes turned to Bill and Abe, who pulled up chairs.

"You are late, *Viejo*," said El Perro.

"Fashionably," said Abe. "How are we getting along?"

"Fashionably," said El Perro with an even bigger grin. "You are a funny man, *Viejo*."

"Glad I amuse you," said Lieberman, looking at the black man in the blue T-shirt. The man wore glasses, had a shaved head and a serious look about him. He couldn't have been more than thirty.

"Want you all to meet my new *abogado*, Jesus Taibo," said El Perro, pointing a thumb at the black man with the brief-case. "Tell them what that means, *Viejo*."

"He's a lawyer," said Lieberman.

In response Jesus Taibo looked at Parker Liao, Mr. Woo, and the two policemen and said, "Is it all right if I take something out of my briefcase?"

"Depends on what it is," said Lieberman.

"A document," said Taibo.

"Carefully," said Abe.

Taibo opened the briefcase and slowly withdrew a small stack of letter-sized white sheets. He handed one to Mr. Woo first and then to Parker Liao, Bill, Abe, and El Perro.

"It's a letter of agreement," said Taibo.

"I sign no letters of agreement," said Parker Liao, placing the sheet on the table without looking at it.

"It can't incriminate you," said Taibo. "It simply says that the undersigned are witnesses to a verbal agreement between two clubs, the Tentaculos and the Twin Dragons, to respect each other's spatial integrity; that space, in each case, is indicated on this map."

Taibo reached into his briefcase again and came out with a map, which he carefully unfolded. The map had two areas of Chicago outlined in black marker.

They all looked at the map.

"You may destroy the map after you have examined it," said Taibo. "In fact, I suggest that you do, but the choice is yours. Paragraph two of the letter states that no member of either club is to enter into any confrontation, verbal or physical, with members of the other club so long as the integrity of the designated areas is respected."

"This means nothing," said Liao, looking at El Perro. "He respects nothing. He is a lunatic."

"Insults degrade the process of negotiation," said Taibo calmly, folding his hands on the table. "Mr. Woo is here to witness this understanding, as are Detectives Lieberman and Hanrahan. We ask Mr. Woo to verify that Mr. Liao has of his own free will agreed to this proposal. We ask further that he accept responsibility for insuring that the Twin Dragons abide by the agreement. We ask that Detective Lieberman do the same for the Tentaculos. Neither of you need sign anything though it would solemnize the ritual commitment of this agreement. However, my client is willing to accept your assurances."

"I sign nothing," said Liao, slowly standing.

"Please sit," said Mr. Woo.

Liao looked at the old man. There was a brief battle of wills but it was clear to Lieberman that the younger man was not prepared to challenge Mr. Woo, not yet, not here.

"I accept this responsibility," said Mr. Woo.

Parker Liao sat. Silence.

"Detective Lieberman?" asked Jesus Taibo.

"Let's put it this way," said Lieberman. "The Tentaculos break the agreement, I break the Tentaculos."

El Perro laughed and clapped his hands.

"What'd I tell you, Taibo? The man has *cojónes*. He means it."

"I sign nothing," said Parker Liao. "I'll give my word, but my signature goes on nothing."

Taibo nodded and collected maps and the copies of the document.

"My client will accept your assurance under the guarantee of Mr. Woo," said Taibo, snapping the clasp on the briefcase after returning the papers to it.

El Perro looked at Abe and raised his eyebrows in pride for the performance of his young lawyer.

"Fuckin' Princeton," said El Perro as Taibo rose.

"I don't think my services are needed here any longer," the lawyer said, adjusting his glasses.

Abe wondered if Taibo would try to shake hands with the men around the table. He hoped the lawyer was too smart for that. Why chance a rebuff?

This time Woo and Abe looked at each other, both understanding that the young lawyer had never expected Parker Liao to sign the document any more than he expected his client to sign. The document really did mean nothing. The agreement was only as good as the respect or fear the two gang leaders had for Woo and Lieberman and their own desire to get out of the possible gang war that would benefit neither of them.

"Suggestion," said Lieberman. "Emiliano, you and Piedras leave now. Parker and his friends will follow in five minutes."

El Perro nodded in agreement, got up, and, with Piedras watching his back, left the room.

Lieberman looked at his watch. Woo sat with hands folded in front on his chest.

"Gentlemen," Lieberman said, looking at the Twin Dragons.

Liao rose slowly, glanced at Woo, who looked at Parker and said, "Did you have that discussion with Mr. Li?"

It was Parker Liao's turn to look at Lieberman.

"He will respond to neither option," said Parker.

Hanrahan suspected that those options were reason and the threat of violence. The conversation between the two men could have been carried on privately. Mr. Woo wanted it to take place in front of Bill Hanrahan.

"We will see," said Woo.

Liao and his two men left the room, closing the door behind them.

"Iris Chen," said Woo. "She is well?"

"My wife is well," said Hanrahan.

"Good," said Woo. "Take care of her. I look forward to the birth of her child."

Hanrahan stared at the old man and decided that he was being sincere.

"I can deal with Jon Li," Hanrahan said.

"Yes," said Woo rising, the chair being pulled back gently, smoothly by Sidney Chao. "Detective Lieberman."

Woo nodded. So did Abe and then Woo was gone. Hanrahan and Lieberman sat alone. There was a knock on the door and Meg Dwyer, plump, bleached-blond, came in and looked around.

"Barney wanted to be sure you were both still alive," she said. "Wanted to know if they'd cut your throats."

"And if they had, Meg?" asked Bill.

"I'd be calling our cleanup man to come in early," she said. "Drink?"

Meg knew that Bill was clean and sober.

"Celebration," said Bill. "I'll have a Coke. Not the careful kind. Caffeine, sugar, the works. Abe?"

"On the house," said Meg.

"Make mine the same," he said. "You only live once or twice or forever."

When Bill got back to the station, he had a visitor, but not in the squad room, in Kearney's office. He went in and found not Kearney but Hugh Morton standing at the window facing him.

"I'm here to thank you," Morton said.

"For . . . ?"

"Wrapping up Berg. I heard what you did."

"With a little help from my partner," Bill said.

"Your quick work may have saved my career," said Morton still standing across the room, arms at his side. "Unless you plan to arrest me for leaving the scene of a crime."

"Let's say you were distraught," said Hanrahan. "Let's say you weren't there."

A pause. Morton looked over his shoulder out the window and then turned back to Hanrahan.

"I wanted to be the one who killed them," said Morton.

"I know," said Bill. "So would I if I were you. How's you wife?"

"She'll be all right," said Morton. "Physically. Mentally . . . You've handled rape cases."

"Yeah. Your boy?"

"I think he'll be all right, too," said Morton, moving around the desk and extending his hand.

Bill took it and they shook.

"I'm heading a new commission," Morton said. "You want a transfer? Good opportunity. Exposure. Recognition, probably promotion if things go well."

"Hitch a ride on your star?" asked Hanrahan.

"Might be a good ride," said Morton.

"I'll think about it," he said as Morton moved past him to the door, but Bill knew he wouldn't think about it.

He didn't need change now. He needed stability. He needed his wife, reasonable hours, Abe and whatever routine his job offered. Maybe he should be ambitious. A new child coming. Maybe he should, but he knew that he wasn't and he was content with that.

Bill checked his watch. He had two hours to get to the airport and pick up Abe's son-in-law.

Abe parked the car alongside the hydrant in front of his house and hurried to the door. The overnight was packed and ready just as Bess had said it would be, just as he knew it would be.

He had a little less than an hour to get to the airport, park, and get on the plane. He wasn't taking his gun. He wouldn't need it and it was too much trouble to get it through security. If he needed one, he could get it from the Yuma police, but he was reasonably certain that it wasn't that kind of trip.

Abe started to go back through the door to his car when he heard the voice of his grandson.

"Grandpa," Barry said.

"Barry, what are you doing home from school?"

"Waiting for you. Grandma said it was all right."

"Your mother?"

Barry shrugged.

"It was all right with her. I want to talk."

The boy looked like his father with just a bit of his mother and a touch of Lieberman's seriousness. At least that's what Abe thought. No one else seemed to see Barry that way.

Abe resisted looking at his watch. He could turn on his flasher, risk his life and weave through traffic. He'd take Touhy and stay off the Expressways and he would hope to make it. Worst that could happen would be a later plane.

"Okay," said Abe, putting down the overnight bag and closing the door behind him. "Let's talk. What are we talking about?"

"I don't think I can have the bar mitzvah," said the boy, sitting heavily on the sofa in the small living room.

"May I ask why?" Lieberman said calmly, sitting next to his grandson.

"I don't believe in God," Barry said.

The chances of making that plane to Yuma had just gotten much slimmer.

When Jon Li made his call to Iris Chen Hanrahan, Bill was on the way to the airport to pick up Abe's son-in-law. Abe was talking to his grandson. El Perro was making his lawyer Jesus Taibo very uncomfortable by offering him the supreme honor of calling the numbers for a few games of bingo on Saturday night. Blue Berg was talking to his lawyer who told him that the good news was that there was no chance of a death sentence in Illinois. Mr. Woo and Parker Liao sat in Mr. Woo's office working out a new, informal relationship between them.

And . . .

In the little snip of an instant that hardly covered any real time and seemed like a dream, Wayne saw the young cowboy drop to the floor and pull something out of his pocket.

Wayne was going to fire again. Maybe he did. He didn't remember. The thump on his chest like someone jabbing him to make a point pushed him back a step. Then something stuck in his throat the way a big vitamin pill did sometimes. He dropped to his knees and felt like coughing and sneezing at the same time. And then Wayne fell forward on his face into shattered glass from the window.

The gun was no longer in his hand. Nothing was in his hand. His head was to his left side. He could see shards and bits of glass forming some kind of figure. He imagined chance or God or his own imagination was starting to make a stained glass window. A flying white horse?

Someone turned him over. He looked up at Lee Cole Carter, who held a little gun in his hand. Lee Cole was shouting, "Call the police."

Wayne wanted to talk but words wouldn't come.

"You crazy son of a bitch," Lee Cole said.

Somewhere far away, maybe as far as Houston, Richie was talking to someone on the phone.

"Hero," Wayne gasped and choked.

Lee Cole brushed some shards of glass from Wayne's face.

"You're no hero," said Lee Cole. "Just be quiet. Police are coming."

"No," said Wayne. "You. You're the hero. Shot it out with a crazy sign painter. Beat him to the draw. All over the news. That gun registered?"

Lee Cole nodded and tilted his cowboy hat back like Kenny Rogers or James Garner.

Wayne wanted to say something else. He wasn't sure what it was, but it didn't matter because he could no longer speak. He closed his eyes. Lee Cole lifted Wayne's head and Wayne suddenly, vividly saw the flying white unicorn and Lee Cole

Carter astride it, cowboy hat in one hand, horse bucking in the clouds.

Someone was breathing into his mouth. Lee Cole was trying to keep him alive. Hero.

It was then that Wayne Czerbiak decided not to die. And he didn't.

Before making his call to Iris, Jon Li engaged in a long, deep meditation. He had completed his work for the day, having sold four vacation packages to Orlando over the phone. Jon Li was good on the phone. He was upbeat, laughed sincerely when a potential client said something humorous even if it was sarcastic, was pleasantly relentless, listened to anything they had to say, which ranged from listing illnesses to complaining about relatives.

Jon Li was good on the phone.

The meditation took place in the center of his room, legs folded under him on the floor, eyes fixed on a new photograph of Li Hongzhi. Time ceased to exist. Space ceased to exist. Jon Li ceased to exist. There was only void. No thoughts. No images. Nothing, not even darkness. It was cleansing. It was refreshing. It was also dangerous, since there were times when Jon did not come out of his meditative state for hours instead of the minutes he had planned on. He had considered some kind of alarm to bring him back to what most of humanity called reality, had even experimented with a gentle buzz on an alarm radio. He had been too deeply into his meditation to react to it. He had tried being brought back by the sound of gentle waves, the singing of whales, the falling of rain. None had worked. And he would not destroy the benefits of his meditation with a loud or harsh sound.

A thought vibrated on the edge of the unknown and began to grow glowing. Consciousness returned and Jon Li breathed deeply, uncrossed his legs, and moved to the telephone. He dialed and Iris answered.

"Have you decided?" he said.

"Jon," she answered calmly. "I am having the phone number changed in the next few hours."

"Then I will find the new number. I know telephones. And if I cannot reach you by phone, I will send you letters and if you do not open them I will appear before you to warn you."

"Jon . . ."

"It is what I must do for you," he said. "It is my responsibility."

"I'm going to tell my father about this," she said. "He will inform your father."

"That does not matter," he said. "Your father and mine are not enlightened."

"If I tell my husband, he will . . ."

"He has already been to see me. As has an emissary from Mr. Woo. It makes no difference. The child cannot be born."

Iris hung up. When it rang again a few seconds later, she ignored it. It kept ringing. She had an answering machine, still in its box from RadioShack, next to the phone. She was going to wait till she had the new phone number, but she decided to do it now. She forced herself to calmly remove the wrapping on the box.

The phone kept ringing.

"You don't have to believe in God to be a Jew," said Lieberman. "It's like an Arab saying he's not an Arab."

"But," said Barry, shifting on the sofa so he could look directly at his grandfather, "it's wrong to have a bar mitzvah without believing in God."

"Thousands of people do it," said Abe. "Consider it a ritual that will please your grandmother. Ritual is terrific stuff if it's done right. And think of all the presents people have bought. And the food, don't forget the food, and the hotel, and . . ."

He didn't add that he himself had gone through his bar mitzvah as a devout atheist. At the time, he thought agnosticism was an act of cowardice.

"I'm not even Jewish," Barry said. "Not really."

"You're not?"

"My father isn't a Jew," Barry said. "My name is Cresswell, not Lieberman."

"Your mother is Jewish," said Lieberman. "Your mother is the one who determines whether you're Jewish or not."

He felt like adding, "just ask the Nazis" but settled for letting the information sink in. A combination of guilt, tradition, and reason were in the lap of his grandson.

"I know those things," Barry said. "My mother doesn't care about being Jewish. She married my father and Dr. Alexander. They're not Jewish."

Lieberman felt like saying, "Marvin Alexander is more Jewish than I am."

Lieberman's son-in-law had studied medicine in Israel,

spoke Hebrew, which Abe did not, read Hebrew, which Abe did but didn't understand, and knew the history and holidays.

"You talk to your father about this?" asked Abe.

Barry nodded.

"He said I couldn't disappoint you and Grandma," Barry said. "But . . . it feels wrong, you know?"

"I know," said Abe. "You want to call it off, I'll talk to your grandmother about calling it off, but think about what that will mean. You ask me, it's a lot easier to go through with it than spend the rest of your life living with the cancellation of your bar mitzvah for ethical reasons. I'm a great believer in ethics, my own ethics, but sometimes a little ethical compromise to make people you love happy is worth doing."

"You wouldn't really ask Grandma to let me out of the bar mitzvah," he said.

"Well, to tell the truth—which I do on a regular-enough basis to make me a more than honest man—no, I wouldn't ask her. What I would ask her, if I fail here and now, is to help me figure out a way to convince you, blackmail you, or bribe you into going through with the bar mitzvah."

"You would bribe me?"

"Not really," Abe said. "I just threw that in with the hope that your imagination would take flight."

"You think I'm just scared," Barry said.

Abe shifted a bit more so that he looked directly at his grandson.

"I think you're scared," said Abe. "I think it would be a little goofy if you weren't."

"Goofy? No one says *goofy*," Barry said with a grin.

"I say *goofy* and *snafu* and *give me some skin* and . . ."

"No you don't," said Barry.

"Well, I'm only committed to being honest half the time, remember?"

"I guess I'm doing it," said Barry with a sigh.

"I guess you are," said Lieberman.

"I guess I just had to say it out loud to someone," he said.

"And," said Lieberman rising and looking at his watch, "I'm honored that you chose me. I've got to go catch a plane to Yuma."

"Arizona?"

"Is there another one?"

Barry stood.

"Do we shake hands now or what?" asked Lieberman.

Barry put his arms around his grandfather and hugged him. Abe hugged back. Barry hugged harder. The kid was strong.

"You'll be back in time tomorrow?" Barry said, still holding Lieberman.

"Wouldn't miss it," Abe said. "Better not. Your grandmother would be perturbed, your mother livid, your granduncle Maish disappointed, Rabbi Wass confused, and a lot of people saying or thinking 'What else did you expect from that goofy Lieberman?' "

"You better get going," said Barry, letting go.

Abe moved to the door and picked up the overnight bag. He looked at his watch. He had less than an hour to make the plane. The airport on a perfect day was forty-five minutes away.

"You're late," said Barry.

"I'll make it. I'll put on my flashing light and weave through traffic. One of the many perks about being a cop. Go to school."

"Too late," he said.

"Then study your speech or your Torah portion."

"Got it down," Barry said, pointing to his head.

Abe always pointed to his head.

"Then do something very mildly evil. Eat a ham sandwich."

Abe waved, closed the door behind him, and hurried down the steps.

Bill had just put Marvin Alexander's leather suitcase in the trunk of his car and gotten in the car when his cell phone rang.

Alexander, tall, broad-shouldered, wearing tan slacks and a tan shirt, settled in.

"Hello," said Bill.

"Bill," Iris said. "You went to see Jon Li."

"Who told you that?"

The pause was long. Hanrahan looked at Marvin Alexander, who was doing a successful job of not looking interested in the conversation.

"He called you again," Hanrahan said.

"Yes, but . . ."

"He won't make another call," said Bill.

"Bill, don't . . ."

"I'm busy now, honey," he said. "I'll call you or get home as soon as I can."

He pushed the *off* button and pocketed the phone.

As he turned on the ignition and looked over his shoulder to back out, Alexander said, "Family problems?"

"What makes you think so?" asked Bill, backing up.

"I don't think you call Abe or any other cop 'honey' and I doubt if you'd call a girlfriend 'honey' in front of me."

"You should have been a detective," said Bill, driving away from the curb where he had parked with his police card showing on the pulled-down sun visor. He left the visor down. He was heading into the sun.

"I am," he said. "You find criminals. I find disease and trauma."

"Doc . . . ," Bill began.

Marvin held up his hands and said, "I hope you're not going to ask me for domestic advice. I think you know enough about my life to know I'm the wrong person. You're Catholic, right?"

"Yeah."

"You have a priest?"

"Yeah. His name is Whizzer."

"Strange name for a priest."

"He's also black."

"Less strange."

"There's something I have to do," Bill said. "Okay if I just drop you at the house? If there's no one there, you know where they hide the key?"

"Lisa told me," said Marvin. "You want to talk, I'll listen."

"No," said Bill. "I've got to *do*, not talk."

He pulled onto the street, almost colliding with a car with a flashing police light on the roof.

"That's Abe," he said, turning his head.

Marvin turned, too, to watch Lieberman screech toward the parking lot.

"Shouldn't we turn back and . . ."

"No," said Bill. "He's on his way to Yuma."

"Yuma?"

"It's a long story," Bill said, driving over the speed limit.

The flight to Yuma was bumpy. Abe didn't like bumpy. In fact, Abe didn't like airplanes. He also didn't like the fact that no one looked particularly worried when turbulence struck. And he didn't like the calm voice of the pilot saying, "As you can see, we are experiencing a little turbulence, so we would appreciate your staying in your seats with your seat belts buckled. We'll resume snack service as soon as we get through this. It should not be long."

The ridiculously thin blond woman next to him was sleeping. The flight was full and Abe got the aisle seat in the next-to-the-last row near the rear restrooms, which was fine with him. He did not sleep on airplanes. He did want the restroom nearby if he needed it.

The Yuma airport wasn't particularly busy and since there were few gates, he found himself walking right past where Gower had been shot and killed by Billy Johnstone.

Abe's carry-on had wheels. He wheeled resolutely forward checking his watch and almost ran into Martin Parsons.

"Sorry I'm late," Parsons said. "Convenience store robbery."

Abe nodded and the two detectives moved toward the exit. That was all Parsons said as they walked until Abe spoke.

"You have a question."

"Yes."

"Your question," Lieberman said, "is what am I doing here? This is your case, your town, and whatever I'm here for you could have taken care of."

"Something like that," Parsons said as they made a turn toward the exit and baggage-claim area.

"If I tell you, you'll have to tell your superior," said Abe. "It can get messy. If you don't know and things go right, I'll be back on a plane tomorrow and you can forget I was even here."

"If things go right," said Parsons.

They moved through glass doors and headed for a marked police car.

"You have the information I asked for?" asked Lieberman.

Parsons pulled out a folded, typed sheet of paper and handed it to Lieberman as they got into the car. Lieberman read the single-spaced report, lips pursed.

"I don't get it," said Parsons.

"Where is Johnstone?"

"Private room, getting better fast, uniformed officer at the door."

"He lawyered?"

"Lawyered up," said Parsons.

Eighteen minutes later Parsons parked the car and said, "Booked you into the same motel."

"Thanks," said Lieberman, getting out of the car.

"I don't suppose you want me up there with you?"

"Your town. Your decision, but I think . . ."

"Never mind," said Parsons. "I'll be right here. I've got a paperback in the glove compartment, new John Lutz. Johnstone's in three-eleven."

Lieberman went through the hospital doors, headed for the elevator, went up and showed his badge to the burly Hispanic cop at the door.

"Been expecting you," the cop said.

"He awake?"

"Last time I looked," said the cop.

Lieberman went into the room and closed the door behind him. Johnstone looked up and smiled. The television set in the corner was on. Peter Strauss was extolling the virtues of Miracle-Gro.

"Didn't get you into too much trouble, did I?" the old man asked.

He was clean-shaven, sitting up and not looking as if he had been shot a few days earlier.

"No," said Lieberman.

"Cubs and St. Louis on in about half an hour," he said. "ESPN. Stay and watch?"

"Don't think so," said Lieberman, pulling a chair next to the bed and sitting at eye level with Johnstone. "Mind turning off the sound for a few minutes?"

Johnstone pressed the *mute* button and there was ambient silence.

"You know why I'm here?" asked Lieberman.

"Came all the way back to makes things tidy. Ask me some questions now that I'm wide-awake and getting on the mend," said Johnstone. "Go ahead. Throw your first pitch."

"It's a curveball, Billy," said Lieberman.

Johnstone waited, eyes wide.

"Throw it."

"You don't have cancer," Lieberman said.

"I most certainly do," said Johnstone. "I'll give you my doctor's name."

"I've got it," said Lieberman. "You had prostate cancer three years ago. Prostate was removed. Your PSA is better than mine. You're not dying."

"Hell," Johnstone said with a chuckle. "We're all dying. You got a point here? I told you I did it for my grandchildren. If I have to go to prison awhile, that's fine. My lawyer says we put it to a judge. My age, health, the guy I killed, he figures I'll do a few years someplace not so bad."

"I think you should call your lawyer before my next curveball."

"No need. No need."

"Your grandchildren don't need your money to go to college," said Lieberman. "It won't hurt but they don't need it. Both of them have full scholarships. Your grandson is both a computer whiz and a pitcher with prospects. Granddaughter is opera material. Talented kids."

"Smart, too," Johnstone said. "Extra cash is good insurance."

The old man's smile was gone now.

"Worth killing for?"

"Depends on who gets killed."

Johnstone looked up at the television screen. The end of a black-and-white movie. Mickey Rooney was talking fast and silently. There was a little bandage over his right eye.

"*The Strip*," said Lieberman. "Pretty good movie. Rooney plays the drums. He was a pretty good drummer."

"Damn good drummer," Johnstone said, clicking off the television. "You know Louis Armstrong, Jack Teagarden, Earl 'Fatha' Hines are in this movie, too?"

"Yeah," said Lieberman. "Want your lawyer now?"

"I need him?"

"Don't know," said Lieberman. "Want to take a chance with me? You can always call me a liar later."

Johnstone looked at the blank screen.

"Anthony Imperioli, the man with the disfigured thumbnail," Lieberman said.

"That his name?" said Johnstone.

Lieberman didn't answer, just looked at Johnstone for a beat before going on.

"Cousin of Joseph Imperioli."

"Joseph Imperioli," Johnstone said, as if trying to place the name.

He shook his head.

"Anthony Imperioli has never been in Yuma," said Lieberman.

"What do you expect him to say?"

"Not what he says that counts," said Lieberman. "It's whether I believe him. I believe him. He definitely wasn't here when you say he generously paid for you to kill Gower."

"He was here," said Johnstone. "Most definitely."

"The money. Where is it?"

"I told you . . ."

Lieberman was shaking his head "no" now.

"No money. You made a lot of mistakes, Billy."

The old man looked away now, lips tight.

"You saw the Imperioli cousins in *Newsweek* magazine, right?" said Lieberman.

"Might," said Johnstone. "Passengers leave magazines, books, all kinds of things in the waiting areas or throw them away."

"Let's talk about Faubus," said Lieberman.

"Faubus?"

"The one who told me he was hired by the man with the bad thumb to keep an eye on me and urge me out of Yuma," said Lieberman. "Cowboy Faubus."

"I recall," said Johnstone.

"He wasn't hired by anyone with a bad thumb, was he?" asked Lieberman.

"I don't know the man," said Billy. "If he says he was, I guess he was. Same guy who hired me to shoot Gower."

"You hired Faubus, Billy. You wanted me to spot him, pick him up, so he could give me the story about the man with the thumb and you could back it up. Billy Johnstone, you are one smart and devious janitor."

"Maybe I should talk to my lawyer?"

"Maybe so," said Lieberman. "But I'm still your best bet. I can have Faubus pulled in. I think he'll tell us a different story this time. Of course, it depends on how good a friend he is or how much you paid him."

Johnstone looked at the policeman for a long, serious moment.

"Good friend, no money," he said.

"My grandson's getting bar mitzvahed tomorrow," said Lieberman.

"That a fact? What is it you say, *mayzel tove?*"

"Something like that. Thanks. Billy, why did you kill Gower?"

"Needed killing," said Johnstone. "You got me. What more you need?"

"The answer to two questions. Who did Gower kill?"

"Lots of people, I hear."

"Who did he kill that you loved?" asked Lieberman, softly.

Johnstone looked at the ceiling and said, "Oh, God."

"Billy?"

"I thought I was going to spend a quiet afternoon watching the Cubs," the old man said.

"Still can," said Lieberman.

"Mind won't be on it," Johnstone said. "Okay. My son, my only son, Ronnie. Good son. Didn't always show good judgment. He told me he owed Imperioli a lot of money. Borrowed it to start a sporting goods store. Store went under. Ronnie couldn't get a job."

"Which Imperioli?"

Johnstone held up his hand and pointed at his thumb.

"Ronnie said a man named Gower came and told him he better pay," said Johnstone. "Beg, borrow, steal, kill, but pay. I didn't have the money to help him. Then he was dead. Ronnie was beat up real bad, beat to pieces, left in an alley. I told the police about what Ronnie had said about Imperioli and Gower, but Ronnie's dead in Boston and the police here thought I was a dumb old fool. Called the Boston police, talked to an officer, not even a detective or nothing. He said he'd pass it on. Didn't even ask me to spell my name. I'm damn sure he didn't write down a damn thing."

"Gower?"

"Saw on the television after he'd been arrested here. His picture was up there. They said he was being taken back to Chicago. Had to be the same Gower. TV said he was wanted for a murder. Had to be the same Gower. God or the devil had put him in Yuma. Don't care which. God or the devil told me this was the one chance I was ever going to get to ease the pain."

"So you got a gun," Lieberman said.

"Had a gun," Johnstone said. "Since Korea. You've got it now. Asked some questions at the airport. Found out when a Chicago police officer was scheduled to take off with a prisoner."

He sat back and let out a big sigh of relief.

"That's the story."

"Tell your lawyer that story," said Lieberman, getting up.

"It's true," said Johnstone.

"Yes. Just tell it to your lawyer. It's better than the one about the man with the thumb and the money. He'll want to take it to a jury. Local law won't want it going to a jury. It'll cost them big and you'll get a slap on the cheek. My guess is local law will make a deal and you won't do much jail time, if any. Especially if you tell the truth before someone else does."

"That a fact?"

"Probably," said Lieberman, putting a hand on the man's

shoulder. "That's the way it would go down in Cook County. Still want to see the Cub game?"

"Why not?" said Johnstone.

"I've got to go down, get my bag and tell the cop who shot you to go home."

"He seems like a nice boy," said Johnstone.

"Yeah, he does."

"If my lawyer says 'yes,' I'll do it."

"He'll say 'yes.'"

"Yeah."

"Be right back," said Lieberman.

The old man clicked the television back on and Lieberman left the room nodding at the Hispanic cop, who was seated in a chair reading a newspaper.

"I'm coming back in a few minutes."

The cop nodded.

"We're going to watch the Cub-Cardinal game. Why don't you join us?"

"Sure," said the cop with a grin.

Parsons was waiting where Abe had left him.

"That didn't take long," the younger cop said. "Getting in?"

"I'm staying for a while," said Lieberman. "I'll catch a cab to the motel."

"Get anywhere with Johnstone?"

Lieberman shrugged.

"He wasn't very talkative. I think he may be more willing to talk to you in the next day or two."

"You think so?" said Parsons warily.

"It's a good possibility. Take care of yourself, Martin," Lieberman said, opening the back door of the car and taking his carry-on.

"You too, Abe."

Lieberman backed away and watched as the marked Yuma police car made a U-turn and headed for the exit.

Now if Sammy Sosa would only have a good day, life would be worth living.

17

On Friday, it rained in Yuma. It rained hard and heavy. Lieberman checked with the airport. Flights were being delayed coming in and out, but the weather was expected to break.

His flight was definitely going to be delayed or even canceled.

Abe checked with the airline and found that if he hurried and the weather held at least at the current level, there was a delayed flight to Los Angeles that stood a good chance of getting out an hour late. Los Angeles was clear and there was a flight from LAX to Chicago that should get him home on time for the Friday services.

The cost was three times the price of his present ticket. Lieberman would have to pay for the ticket on his and Bess's American Express card. He gave the ticket clerk his credit card information, hung up, prayed some Indian nearby wasn't doing a rain dance, and called for a cab. They were all busy. He called Martin Parsons.

"Give a fellow officer a ride to the airport?" Lieberman asked.

"It can be done. When?"

"Now would be fine."

"Johnstone and his lawyer want to see me," said Parsons.

"Yeah."

"I'll be right there providing I don't get washed away into the desert."

Twenty minutes later, Parsons pulled in front of the motel and pushed open the passenger-side door, and Lieberman made his dash.

"Normally I would have made it in about eight minutes. How'd the Cubs do yesterday?" Parsons asked.

"Lost. Sammy went zero for three. Kerry Woods came out early," said Lieberman.

"Sorry," said Parsons over the slamming of rain and the rubber squishing of the windshield wipers.

"I'm a Cub fan," said Lieberman. "We live lives of quiet desperation."

They sped through the streets. Lieberman checked his watch. It would be close.

Jon Li had thought it over and come to a decision. Phone calls would not work. Letters would not work. Threats, he was sure, would not work and he had decided it was almost certainly useless to appear at his cousin Iris's door and hope to come up with an irrefutable argument that would persuade her.

He dressed casually, but neatly. Dark slacks. White shirt. Black silk zippered jacket. He brushed his short hair straight back, checked his teeth, and took in a deep breath.

It was a matter of faith. The truth was self-evident but

faith was required to accept it. Iris had no faith except, perhaps, in the Buddhism she and most of Li's family clung to.

The doorbell rang.

He checked the fishing knife with the long, folding blade that lay on the sink in front of him. He closed the blade and put the knife in his pocket.

The doorbell rang.

Jon Li turned out the bathroom light and moved across the bedroom to the living room where he looked at the photograph of Li Hongzhi.

The doorbell rang.

He went to the door and opened it. It wouldn't have surprised him if it had been any of several people, but this was someone he had not expected, certainly someone he had not expected to see at his door with a gun in hand.

He smiled and the bullet smashed into his right eye, went through his brain, crashed through his skull, and fell to the floor and for an instant Jon Li truly felt that for the first time he had levitated.

Sean O'Neil had a headache.

He sat in the hospital waiting to talk to Wayne Czerbiak, who, the Indian doctor named Pordpie or something like that said, would almost certainly live.

O'Neil had decided more than an hour ago that there were many things wrong with being a cop. The long hours. The pay. The things he had to do and see. The people he had to work with. The people he had to work against, but the worst, the all-time definite worst, was the waiting, the sitting around and waiting, waiting in cars on stakeouts, waiting at the phone for a call, and waiting in hospitals.

The attempt on the life of Carter was big news. The hero

of the hour was the country singer, not O'Neil, who had arrived a few seconds too late.

Lee Cole Carter had a permit to carry a concealed weapon. Lee Cole Carter, *Maverick* hat tilted back on his head, had beaten stupid Wayne Czerbiak to the draw.

It would sell an extra few million albums.

Sean O'Neil would get reamed because he had been a few seconds late and because he was Sean O'Neil and there were few in the world who liked Sean O'Neil and none in the world who loved him.

He didn't feel sorry for himself. He just felt pissed. He should check with Hanrahan and see how the Morton case was going. If Morton was brought down, Sean would feel better about the day.

The hospital waiting room smelled like iodine and disinfectant.

The television set in the waiting room wasn't working. Sean should have brought a book, but he didn't.

Barry was just moving to the bimah as the cantor finished chanting the first prayer. Rabbi Wass sat, *tallis* over his shoulders, right behind the table on which the Torah scroll would be opened the next morning for Barry and the others who would be reading a section on Noah's preparation of the Ark.

The chapel was almost full and Rabbi Wass had started the evening with a special word about Ida Katzman.

In the front row sat Bess, Barry's younger sister Melissa, Lisa and her husband Marvin, Maish and his wife Yetta. Next to them were Barry's father, Todd Creswell, and his wife Gail. The *alter cockers* were scattered through the chapel, and seated in the rear were Hanrahan and Iris. Howie Chen had joined them.

Morrie Greenblatt, as he had for several hundred bar and

bat mitzvahs over the decades, gathered those who were to read, speak, open and close the ark, and carry the Torah. He showed them where to sit and indicated to them when it was their turn to move forward and perform their task. He did it smoothly, calmly, without effort and with the certainty that in spite of the anxiety of the family, the evening and the next day would pass without major problems.

Abe entered from the rear and moved forward knowing all eyes were on him. He had parked in the driveway of the temple. He had run in hearing the cantor's voice and knowing that he had just barely made it on time.

As he passed Herschel Rosen, seated on the aisle, Rosen said, "You lost me four dollars to Hurwitz. I said you wouldn't make it."

Abe spotted Hanrahan as he moved. He nodded. Bill nodded back. Abe felt something wrong in his partner's forced smile, but he didn't have time to think about it. Bess moved over to make room for him and handed him a Siddur, a prayer book. Lisa gave him a disapproving look but her husband Marvin gave him a nod that said everything was all right. Melissa took his hand and Barry, on the bimah, gave him a smile before beginning to lead the prayer service.

"You were not perfect," Abe said to his grandson a little over an hour later, a slice of carrot cake before each of them. "You were better than perfect."

"Tomorrow's the hard part," Barry said, taking a forkful of cake.

"No, the hard part is the beginning. It's over."

People approached their table and gave their congratulations. No presents were given in the temple. Presents would come tomorrow, Saturday, at the dinner, when the rite of passage was complete.

The room off of the chapel was not huge but it was big

enough for the table of cakes and pastries and the containers of decaf coffee. There was also a punch bowl and two flavors of ice cream being served by members of the women's club of the synagogue.

"Okay if I go sit with my friends?" Barry asked.

"Go," said Bess, with a smile.

"I'm most definitely Jewish," Barry said.

"Most definitely," Abe agreed.

"Only one slice, Abe," Bess whispered.

"One," Abe said, looking down at his carrot cake. He would save the icing part with the orange-icing carrot for the end.

"He was good," said Marvin Alexander across the table, touching Lisa's hand.

Lisa looked around knowing that almost everyone knew she was married to the good-looking black man holding her hand. Normally, she would have met the eyes of anyone whom she caught staring at them, met them with defiance, but not tonight. Lisa Lieberman Alexander was in a very good mood.

She smiled and said, "He was good. I was afraid you weren't going to make it, Abe."

"God parted the clouds, stopped the rain, and sent a dove with a sprig of green," said Abe.

"You were lucky," said Maish. "He could have shot you out of the sky with a bolt of lightning. He does things like that."

"Maish," said his wife Yetta. "Give it a rest already."

"Sorry," said Maish.

Rabbi Wass had carefully avoided the older Lieberman brother and was now standing near the punch bowl, ready to make a move toward another group if Maish decided the time was ripe for a rant against God.

Lieberman looked around for Hanrahan and Iris and saw them at the door about to leave.

"Be right back," he told Bess, got up and wove his way through small clusters of congratulating people.

"It's early, Father Murph," said Lieberman, catching up with Bill.

"Long day, Rabbi," said Hanrahan. "Iris is getting tired."

"Lovely service," Iris said.

Lieberman took her hand.

"Back tomorrow?"

"Crack of nine," said Hanrahan.

"You can come at ten," said Abe. "Won't miss anything. You okay, Father Murph?"

"Been better. Been worse. Need some sleep."

Iris took her husband's hand and leaned against him.

"See you tomorrow," said Abe.

He stood in the hallway and watched them walk down to the door and out past an off-duty cop named Tyner who was providing security. Lieberman went back to the table and discovered that the icing he had been holding till the end was gone, carrot and all.

"Not me," Bess said.

Lieberman turned to his granddaughter. Melissa smiled. He touched her cheek.

"This calls for negotiation," he said to his wife. "One *ruggalah*."

"One," she conceded.

"I'll get it," said Melissa and hurried away.

On Saturday, Abe learned of the murder of Jon Li. On Saturday, following a service as good or better than the one the night before, there was a party at the Jewish War Veterans' meeting hall.

The presents were piled on a table at the entrance and envelopes with money were handed to Abe, who stuffed them into his pockets till his pockets were full. Then Bess took them.

Rabbi Wass's cousin Leo had a klezmer band. They danced, sang, and made a mess till a few minutes before midnight. Melissa had long since fallen asleep on a couch in the JWV office.

An hour later Marvin and Lisa said good night and went up the stairs of the house on Jarvis. Marvin carried the sleeping Melissa in his arms.

"Can we open the presents now?" Barry asked.

"First thing in the morning," said Bess. "Promise. We want your sister to see. And we got her a present, too."

"Tomorrow," said Barry, resigned. "Good night."

"You were terrific," said Abe. "But I already told you that fifteen or twenty times."

Barry waved and moved up the stairs.

"Tired?" Abe asked Bess.

"Am I tired? Am I human? Of course I'm tired. A cup of decaf?"

"Why not?" he said, moving to the kitchen.

"Who is Mr. Woo?" asked Bess. "He sent a present."

"You got an hour?"

"I've got till we finish coffee," she said.

There were also presents from Captain Kearney, who had been invited but had not come; from El Perro; and from a variety of cops all over the city.

"Abe?"

"Yes."

"In two years Melissa will be ready for her bat mitzvah."

"Couldn't happen to a nicer child. Thanks for reminding

me. I'll sleep better tonight knowing that we've got to start planning for it next year."

They sat at the kitchen table waiting for the coffee to heat.

"Next year?" said Bess. "Make that next month."

18

As Bess Lieberman poured two cups of coffee in her kitchen . . .

Mr. Woo sat in his bedroom still fully dressed and looked at the small, rough stone bust of a human head that sat on a three-hundred-year-old dark enameled table. The bust was at least five thousand years older than the table. He reached out and touched the rough surface of the bust and said something, but what he said was so quiet that even had someone been in the room they would not have heard what the old man said.

Hugh Morton sat in a chair next to the bed looking at his wife. There was one light on, a small night-light. She seemed to be sleeping peacefully but every once in a while she let out a tiny sound like just a little bit of air escaping a balloon. When he heard the sound, he leaned forward and touched her brow. Her hair was moist with perspiration. He whispered and had someone been in the room they would have heard him say, "I'm here."

Billy Johnstone sat up in a hospital chair in Yuma in darkness except for the light from the television set on which a rerun of *Wagon Train* was playing. The rain drummed against the window. The second day of rain. He found it restful. He shifted slightly and with more than a little discomfort to reach into the pocket of his robe and remove his wallet. He flipped it open to the photograph of his son Ronnie. Ronnie was smiling in the photograph. Billy touched the photograph with a single finger, closed the wallet slowly, and returned it to his pocket.

Bill Hanrahan sat in his kitchen. He had left Iris asleep upstairs and now he sat thinking about how he had sat on so many nights at this very table, a bottle of whiskey in front of him, memories clouding the room, memories that needed to be exorcised. He knew he wasn't going to drink. No more. No matter what. But he couldn't help thinking. It was the price he had to pay and he was prepared to pay it. He was examining the backs of his hands, seeing the few brown spots that had begun to appear, when he was aware of Iris at the doorway. He hadn't heard her but he sensed her there. She looked lovely.

"Bill, we should talk."

He nodded. They talked. And Iris told her husband that she had been the one who killed Jon Li.

Morrie Greenblatt leaned over to pick up a napkin the cleaning crew had missed on Friday night. He was alone in the temple. He liked being alone in the temple, particularly in the chapel.

He dropped the napkin into the trash container and moved into the chapel. The small perpetual lights next to the names of dead congregants etched on a bronze tablet glowed softly. Morrie shambled over to the tablet and reached out to touch the slightly warm bulb next to the name of his beloved wife. He uttered her name, and for a reason he didn't understand and didn't examine, a memory returned of a morning minyan thirty years ago at the old shul. They had been one man short of the ten needed and Morrie had found an old man in the hall and brought him to the service, a service marked by an intruding gunman. The tenth man had turned out not to be a Jew, but God had apparently forgiven Morrie for his mistake and had allowed the former tile salesman a long and reasonably contented and useful life. It was late. Morrie sighed and moved to the chapel door. He turned, looked around to be sure that everything was all right, and said, "Amen."